THE HAUNTED FLUTE
AND OTHER JAPANESE STORIES

THE HAUNTED FLUTE
AND OTHER JAPANESE STORIES

Illustrated by Warwick Goble

Derrydale Books
New York · Avenel

Published by Derrydale Books, distributed by
Random House Value Publishing, Inc.
40 Engelhard Avenue, Avenel, New Jersey 07001

Random House
New York • Toronto • London • Sydney • Auckland

Designed by Liz Trovato
Edited by Nina Rosenstein
Production supervised by Ellen Reed

Printed and bound in Singapore

Library of Congress Cataloging-in-Publication Data
The haunted flute and other Japanese stories / illustrated by Warwick Goble.
p. cm.
Summary: A collection of traditional Japanese folktales, including
"The Magic Teakettle," "Urashima," "The Tongue-Cut Sparrow,"
and "Momotaro, Son of the Peach."
ISBN 0-517-12216-2
1. Fairy tales—Japan. 2. Tales—Japan. [1. Fairy tales.
2. Folklore—Japan.] I. Goble, Warwick, ill.
PZ8.H2942 1995
398.2'0952—dc20
94-24737
CIP
AC

8 7 6 5 4 3 2 1

Contents

Introduction

LET us spin the globe and take a trip across space and time to the other side of the world, to old Japan. Back then, the fairies were not as shy as they are today. That was a time when animals could talk to people, when spells and enchantments and magic were always in the air, when there was lots of hidden treasure, and adventures for the asking.

In this collection of traditional folk tales that are most loved by Japanese boys and girls, you will find adventures and enchantments aplenty. In "The Haunted Flute," for example, a young girl finds a supernatural way to contact her beloved father. In "The Magic Teakettle," you'll meet a delightful teakettle that not only sings and dances but is very wise. And in "The Jellyfish Takes a Journey," you will learn why the jellyfish has no bones.

In all these stories, good, simple people are rewarded with love or riches or the child they always wanted. But greedy and jealous folks had better watch out—for they invariably find themselves getting just what they deserve. That's why you won't pity the nasty, envious neighbors in "Hana-Saka-Jiji" or the selfish old woman in the tale about the tongue-cut sparrow. You'll see that promises are to be kept—not broken—and those who forget must suffer the consequences. Your spine may tingle when you read about the bewitching Cold Lady or the eerie story of the Sword of Idé.

 7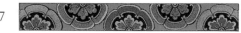

You may laugh when you discover that an ordinary mirror can bring amazement as well as confusion to an entire community—but neither the simple farmer and his wife in "Reflections" nor the country family in "The Matsuyama Mirror" had ever before seen a mirror, or even their own reflections.

Japanese folklore has its own Rip Van Winkle, as you'll learn when you read about Urashima, a fisherman. And you'll see how the fairies' mallet can grant any wish—and can even teach a jealous brother a lesson.

So sit back now and enjoy these tales of ghosts and gods from old Japan. Let yourself drift into the dreamlike, poetic world of these stories, where truth and trickery sometimes intermingle and miracles happen every day.

8

The Haunted Flute

THERE once lived in Yedo a kind man whose wife was gentle and loving. They had one child, a daughter, whom they called O'Yoné, which means "Rice in the ear." Each of them loved this child more than life. And the child grew up to be a lovely young girl, as straight and slender as the green bamboo.

When O'Yoné was twelve years old, her mother grew ill, and before the red had faded from the leaves of the maples she was dead and buried in the earth. The husband was wild in his grief. He cried aloud, he beat his breast, he lay upon the ground and refused comfort, and for days he neither ate nor slept. The child was quite silent.

Time passed. The man had to attend to his business. The snows of winter fell and covered his wife's grave. The worn pathway from his house to the graveyard was also covered with snow, undisturbed except for the faint prints of a child's sandaled feet. In the springtime the man planted the orange lily of forgetfulness, and thought of his wife no more. But the child remembered.

Before the year passed, he brought a new bride home, a woman with a fair face and a black heart. But the man, poor fool, was happy, and praised his child to her and believed that all was well.

Now because her father loved O'Yoné, her stepmother hated her with a jealous and deadly hatred, and was nasty and cruel to the

child, whose gentle ways and patience only angered her more. But because of the father's presence she did not dare to do O'Yoné any great harm. She waited, biding her time. The poor child passed her days and her nights in torment and horrible fear. But she said not a word of this to her father.

Now, after some time, O'Yoné's father was called away on business to the distant city of Kyoto. From Yedo it was many days' journey on foot or on horseback. The evening before his departure, which was to be very early in the morning, he called O'Yoné to him and said, "Come here, my dear little daughter." So O'Yoné went and knelt before him.

"What gift shall I bring you home from Kyoto?" he said.

She hung her head and did not answer.

"Answer, then, little one," he insisted. "Shall it be a golden fan, or a roll of silk, or a new *obi* of red brocade?"

O'Yoné burst into bitter tears, and her father took her upon his knees to soothe her. But she hid her face with her sleeves and cried as if her heart would break. "Oh Father, Father, Father," she said, "do not go away—do not go away!"

"But, my sweet, I must," he answered, "and soon I shall be back—so soon, it will scarcely seem that I am gone, when I shall be here again with fair gifts in my hand."

"Father, take me with you," she said.

"Alas, what a great journey for a little girl! Will you walk on your feet, my little pilgrim, or mount a packhorse? And how would you fare in the inns of Kyoto? No, my dear, stay. It is but for a short time, and your kind mother will be with you."

She shuddered in his arms. "Father, if you go, you will never see me again."

Then the father felt a sudden chill about his heart. But he would not listen. What! Must he, a grown man, be swayed by a child's fancies? He put O'Yoné gently down, and she slipped away as silently as a shadow.

In the morning she came to him before sunrise. In her hand was a little flute made of bamboo and smoothly polished. "I made it myself," she said, "from a bamboo in the grove that is behind our garden. I made it for you. As you cannot take me with you, take the little flute, honorable father. Play on it sometimes, and think of me." Then she wrapped the flute in a scarf of white silk, lined with scarlet, and wound a scarlet cord around it. She gave it to her father, who put it in his kimono sleeve. After this he departed, taking the road to Kyoto. As he went he looked back three times and saw his child standing at the gate, watching him. Then the road turned and he saw her no more.

The city of Kyoto was exciting and beautiful. And what with his business during the day, and his partying in the evenings, time passed merrily for O'Yoné's father, and he gave little thought to Yedo, to his home, or to his child. Two months passed, and three, and he made no plans to return.

One evening he was getting ready to go out to a great dinner with friends; as he searched in his drawer for a certain silken garment that he wished to wear, he came upon the little flute, which had been hidden all this time in the sleeve of his traveling clothes. He unwrapped it from its red and white scarf, and as he did so, he felt strangely cold with an icy chill that crept about his heart. Like one in a dream, he put the flute to his lips, and there came from it a long drawn-out wail.

He dropped the flute hastily upon the floor. He clapped his hands for his servant, and told him he would not go out that night. He was not well; he wished to be alone. After a long time he reached out his hand for the flute. Again that long, melancholy cry. He shook from head to foot, but he blew into the flute. "Come back to Yedo . . . come back to Yedo. . . . Father! Father!" The quavering childish voice rose to a shriek and then was silent.

A horrible foreboding now took hold of the man. He rushed from the house and from the city, and journeyed day and night, denying

 12

himself sleep and food. So pale was he and wild that the people he met deemed him a madman and fled from him. At last he came to his journey's end, travel-stained from head to heel, with bleeding feet and half-dead from weariness.

His wife met him at the gate.

He said, "Where is my child?"

"The child?" she answered.

"Ay, the child—my child . . . where is she?" he cried in agony.

The woman laughed. "Now, my lord, how should I know? She is inside studying, or she is in the garden, or she is asleep, or perhaps she has gone out with her playmates, or . . ."

"Enough. No more of this," he said. "Come, where is my child?"

Then she was afraid. "In the Bamboo Grove," she said, looking at him with wide eyes.

There the man ran, and looked for O'Yoné among the green stems of the bamboos. But he did not find her. He called, "Yoné! Yoné!" and again, "Yoné! Yoné!" But he got no answer; only the wind sighed in the dry bamboo leaves.

Then he felt in his sleeve and brought out the little flute. Very tenderly he put it to his lips. There was a faint sighing sound. Then a voice spoke, thin and pitiful: "Father, dear Father, my wicked stepmother killed me. Three months ago she killed me. She buried me in the clearing of the Bamboo Grove. You may find my bones. As for me, you will never see me again—you will never see me again. . . ."

With his own two-handed sword the man did justice, and killed his wicked wife, in revenge for the death of his innocent child. Then he dressed himself in the clothing of mourning and set out upon a pilgrimage to the holy places of Japan.

And he carried the little flute with him, in a fold of his garment, next to his heart.

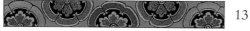
13
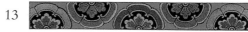

The Jellyfish Takes a Journey

ONCE upon a time the jellyfish was a very handsome fellow. He was beautiful, and as round as the full moon. He had glittering scales and fins and a tail like other fishes, and he even had little feet so he could walk upon the land as well as swim in the sea. He was merry and he was gay, he was beloved and trusted by the Dragon King. In spite of all this, his grandmother always said he would come to a bad end, because he would not pay attention to his books at school. She was right. It all came about in this way.

The Dragon King was newly married when the young Lady Dragon, his wife, became very sick. She took to her bed and stayed there, and wise folk in Dragonland shook their heads and said her last day was at hand. Doctors came from far and near, and they tried every treatment and medicine, but nothing seemed to cure the poor young thing.

The Dragon King was beside himself.

"Heart's Desire," he said to his pale bride, "I would give my life for you."

"Little good would it do me," she answered. "However, if you will fetch me a monkey's liver I will eat it and live."

"A monkey's liver!" cried the Dragon King. "A monkey's liver! You talk wildly, oh light of mine eyes. How shall I find a monkey's

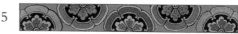

liver? Don't you know, sweet one, that monkeys live in the trees of the forest, while we are here in the deep sea?"

Tears ran down the Dragon Queen's lovely face.

"If I do not have the monkey's liver, I shall die," she said.

Then the Dragon went out and called the jellyfish.

"The Queen must have a monkey's liver," he said, "to cure her of her sickness."

"What will she do with the monkey's liver?" asked the jellyfish.

"Why, she will eat it," said the Dragon King.

"Oh!" said the jellyfish.

"Now," said the King, "you must go and fetch me a live monkey. I have heard that they live in the tall trees of the forest. Therefore swim quickly, my jellyfish, and bring a monkey back with you."

"How will I get the monkey to come along with me?" asked the jellyfish.

"Tell him of all the beauties and pleasures of Dragonland. Tell him he will be happy here and that he may play with mermaids all day long."

"Well," said the jellyfish, "I'll tell him that."

Off set the jellyfish. He swam and he swam until at last he reached the shore where the tall trees of the forest grew. And, sure enough, there was a monkey sitting in the branches of a persimmon tree, eating persimmons.

The very thing, said the jellyfish to himself. I'm in luck.

"Noble monkey," he said, "please will you come to Dragonland with me?"

"How will I get there?" asked the monkey.

"Just sit on my back," said the jellyfish, "and I'll take you there. You'll have no trouble at all."

"Why should I go there, after all?" asked the monkey. "I am very well off as I am."

"Ah," said the jellyfish, "it's plain that you know little of all the beauties and pleasures of Dragonland. There you will be happy as the

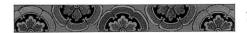 16

day is long. You will win great riches and honor. Besides, you may play with the mermaids from morning until night."

"I'll come," said the monkey.

And he slipped down from the persimmon tree and jumped onto the jellyfish's back.

When the two of them were about halfway to Dragonland, the jellyfish laughed.

"Now, jellyfish, why do you laugh?"

"I laugh for joy," said the jellyfish. "When you come to Dragonland, my master, the Dragon King, will get your liver, and give it to my mistress the Dragon Queen to eat, and then she will recover from her sickness."

"My liver?" asked the monkey.

"Why, of course," said the jellyfish.

"Alas and alack," cried the monkey. "I'm grieved indeed, but if it's my liver you're wanting I haven't got it with me. To tell you the truth, it weighs so much that I just took it out and hung it upon a branch of that persimmon tree where you found me. Quick, quick, let's go back for it."

Back they went, and the monkey was up in the persimmon tree in a twinkling.

"Mercy me, I don't see it at all," he said. "Where can I have mislaid it? I should not be surprised if some rascal has stolen it," he said.

Now if the jellyfish had minded his books at school, would he have been hoodwinked by the monkey? Probably not. But his grandmother always said he would come to a bad end.

"I shall be some time finding it," said the monkey. "You'd best be getting home to Dragonland. The King would not want you to be out after dark. You can call for me another day. *Sayonara*."

The monkey and the jellyfish parted on the best of terms.

The minute the Dragon King set eyes on the jellyfish, he asked, "Where's the monkey?"

 17

"I'm to call for him another day," said the jellyfish. And he told the story.

The Dragon King flew into a towering rage. He called his executioners and ordered them to beat the jellyfish.

"Break every bone in his body," he cried. "Beat him to a jelly."

Alas for the sad fate of the jellyfish! Jelly he remains to this very day.

As for the young Dragon Queen, she laughed and laughed when she heard the story. And the laughter did her good.

"If I can't have a monkey's liver I must do without it," she said. "Give me my best brocade gown and I will get up, for I feel a good deal better."

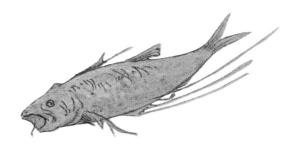

 18

Son of the Thunder God

FOLKS say that Rai-den, the Thunder God, is an unloving spirit, fearful and revengeful, cruel to humankind. These are people who are mortally afraid of the storm, and who hate lightning and tempest. They speak only evil of Rai-den and of Rai-Taro, his son. But they are wrong.

Rai-den Sama lived in a Castle of Cloud set high in the blue heaven. He was a great and mighty god. Rai-Taro was his one and only son, a brave boy, and his father loved him.

In the cool of the evening Rai-den and Rai-Taro would look down from the Castle of Cloud and study the humans upon the earth below.

One night Rai-den Sama said to Rai-Taro, "Child, take a good look tonight at the people below."

Rai-Taro answered, "Father, I will look well."

Together they looked to the north and saw great lords and soldiers in battle. To the south they saw priests in a holy temple. To the east they saw a garden with a fair princess, and a troop of maidens making music for her. There were children there, too, playing with a little cart of flowers.

"Ah, the pretty children!" said Rai-Taro.

To the west they saw a peasant toiling in a rice field. He was weary

and his back ached. His wife worked with him. They were very poor and their clothing was ragged.

"Have they no children?" asked Rai-Taro.

Rai-den shook his head. "Have you looked well, Rai-Taro?" he asked. "Have you looked well tonight upon the doings of the humans below?"

"Father," said Rai-Taro, "indeed, I have looked well."

"Then choose, my son, choose, for I am sending you to live upon the earth."

"Must I go among people?" asked Rai-Taro.

"My child, you must."

"I will not go with the soldiers," said Rai-Taro, "for I do not like fighting."

"Will you go, then, to the garden of the fair princess?"

"No," said Rai-Taro. "I am a man. But neither will I have my head shaved to go and live with priests."

"What, then? Do you choose the poor peasant? You will have a hard life and little to eat, Rai-Taro."

Rai-Taro said, "They have no children. Perhaps they will be happy to love me."

"Go, go in peace," said Rai-den Sama, "for you have chosen wisely."

"How shall I go, my father?" said Rai-Taro.

"Honorably," said his father, "as it befits a Prince of High Heaven."

Now the poor peasant worked in his rice field, which was at the foot of the mountain in Haku-san, in the province of Ichizen. Day after day and week after week the bright sun shone. The rice field was dry, and young rice was burned up.

"Alack and alas!" cried the poor peasant, "what shall I do if my rice crop fails? May the dear gods have mercy on all poor people!"

With that he sat down on a stone at the rice field's edge and fell asleep from weariness and sorrow.

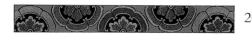 

When he woke the sky was black with clouds. It was noontime, but it grew as dark as night. The leaves of the trees shuddered together and the birds stopped singing.

"A storm, a storm!" cried the peasant. "The Thunder God Rai-den Sama goes abroad upon his black horse, beating the great drum of the Thunder. We shall have rain aplenty, thanks be."

Rain aplenty, he had, sure enough, for it fell in torrents, with blinding lightning and roaring thunder.

"Oh, Rai-den Sama," said the peasant. "Your Greatness, this is even more than enough."

At this the bright lightning flashed anew and struck the earth in a ball of fire, and the heavens cracked with a mighty peal of thunder.

"Ai! Ai!" cried the poor peasant. "This is the end of me." And he lay on the ground and hid his face.

But the Thunder God spared him, and soon he sat up and rubbed his eyes. The ball of fire from the lightning was gone, but a baby lay upon the wet earth—a fine fresh boy with the rain on his cheeks and his hair.

Overjoyed by this living gift from the Thunder God, the poor peasant man scooped up the boy in his arms and carried him to his own home.

As he went the rain still fell, but the sun came out in the blue sky, and every flower in the cooler air lifted up its grateful head.

The peasant came to his cottage door. "Wife, wife," he called, "I have brought something home."

"What may it be?" asked his wife.

The man answered, "It is Rai-Taro, the little eldest son of the Thunder God."

Rai-Taro grew up straight and strong, the tallest, happiest boy in all the countryside. He was the delight of his foster parents, and all the neighbors loved him. When he was ten years old he worked in the rice fields like a man. He was wonderful at predicting the weather.

21

"My father," he would say, "let us do this and that, for we shall have fair weather"; or, "My father, let us instead do this or that, for tonight there will be a storm," and whatever he said, sure enough, it came to pass. And he brought great good fortune to the poor peasant, and all his works prospered.

When Rai-Taro was eighteen years old all the neighbors were invited to his birthday feast. There was plenty of good *saké,* and everyone was merry; only Rai-Taro was silent and sad and sorry.

"What's wrong, Rai-Taro?" asked his foster mother. "You are usually full of laughter and fun; why today are you silent, sad, and sorry?"

"It is because I must leave you," Rai-Taro said.

"No," said his foster mother, "never leave us, Rai-Taro, my son. Why would you leave us?"

"Mother, because I must," said Rai-Taro in tears.

"You have been our great good fortune; you have given us all things. What have I given you? What have I given you, Rai-Taro, my son?"

Rai-Taro answered, "Three things you have taught me—to work hard, to suffer, and to love. I am more learned than the Immortals."

Then he rose up toward the blue heaven on a white cloud until he reached his father's castle. And Rai-den welcomed him. The two of them stood at the Castle of Cloud and looked down to the west at the earth.

The foster mother stood weeping bitterly, and her husband took her hand.

And Rai-Taro called down through the clouds, "Don't cry, Mother. I'll come back someday."

 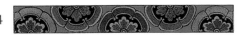

Reflections

LONG ago there lived within a day's journey of the city of Kyoto a gentleman of simple mind and manners, but well-to-do. His wife had been dead for many years, and the good man lived in great peace and quiet with his only son. They kept clear of women, and knew nothing at all of their ways. They had good steady menservants in their house, and from morning until night they never set eyes on a pair of long kimono sleeves or a woman's scarlet *obi*.

The truth is that they were as happy as can be. Sometimes they worked in the rice fields. Other days they went fishing. In the spring, they went out to admire the cherry flower or the plum, or whatever flower was in bloom. At these times they would drink a little *saké* and be as jolly as you please. Often they came home by lantern light late at night. They wore their oldest clothes, and ate whenever they felt like it, even if it wasn't mealtime.

But the pleasures of life are fleeting, and presently the father felt old age creeping upon him.

One night, as he sat smoking and warming his hands over the fire, he said, "Boy, it's high time you got married."

"Now the gods forbid!" cried the young man. "Father, what makes you say such terrible things? Or are you joking? You must be joking," he said.

"I'm not joking at all," said the father. "I never spoke a truer word."

"But, Father, I am mortally afraid of women."

"And am I not also?" asked the father. "I'm sorry for you, my boy."

"Then why must I marry?" asked the son.

"In the way of nature I shall die before long, and you'll need a wife to take care of you."

Now tears filled the young man's eyes when he heard this, for he was tenderhearted; but all he said was, "I can take care of myself very well."

"That's the very thing you cannot do," said his father.

The long and short of it was that they found the young man a wife. She was young, and as pretty as a picture. Her name was Tassel.

After they had drunk the ceremonial cup of wine together and so became man and wife, they stood alone, the young man looking hard at the girl. For the life of him he did not know what to say to her. He took a bit of her sleeve and stroked it with his hand. Still he said nothing and looked mighty foolish. The girl turned red, turned pale, turned red again, and burst into tears.

"Honorable Tassel, don't do that, for the dear gods' sake," said the young man.

"I suppose you don't like me," sobbed the girl. "I suppose you don't think I'm pretty."

"My dear," he said, "you're prettier than the bean flower in the field; you're prettier than the little hen in the farmyard; you're prettier than the rose carp in the pond. I hope you'll be happy with my father and me."

At this she laughed a little and dried her eyes. "Get on another pair of pants," she said, "and give me those you've got on you; there's a great hole in them—I was noticing it all the time of the wedding!"

Well, this was not a bad beginning, and taking one thing with another they got along pretty well, though of course things were not

 26

as they had been in that blessed time when the young man and his father did not set eyes upon a pair of long sleeves or an *obi* from morning until night.

By and by, the old man died. He left his son great wealth, which made him the richest man in the countryside. But this was no comfort at all to the poor young man, who mourned his father with all his heart. Day and night he sat by his father's grave, getting little sleep or rest. He paid little attention to his wife, Mistress Tassel, and her whimsies, or even to the delicious food she set before him. He grew thin and pale, and she, poor thing, was at her wits' end to know what to do with him. At last she said, "My dear, how would it be if you were to go to Kyoto for a little?"

"And why should I do that?" he asked.

It was on the tip of her tongue to answer, "To enjoy yourself," but she saw it would never do to say that.

"Oh," she said, "as a kind of a duty. They say every man that loves his country should see Kyoto; and besides, you might give an eye to the new fashions, so as to tell me what they are like when you get home. My things," she said, "are sadly old-fashioned. I'd like to know what people are wearing."

"I've no heart to go to Kyoto," said the young man, "and if I had, it's the planting time of the rice, and I haven't got time to go and that's that."

All the same, after two days he asked his wife to get out his best clothes and to pack some food for a journey. "I'm thinking of going to Kyoto," he told her.

"Well, I am surprised," said Mistress Tassel. "And what put such an idea into your head, if I may ask?"

"I've been thinking it's a kind of duty," said the young man.

"Oh, indeed," said Mistress Tassel to this, and nothing more. And the next morning she packed her husband off bright and early for Kyoto.

The young man stepped out along the road, feeling a little better,

and before long he reached Kyoto. There he saw many wonderful places—temples and palaces, castles and gardens, and fine streets of shops. He gazed about with his eyes wide open, and his mouth too, most likely, for he was a simple soul.

One fine day he came upon a shop full of metal mirrors that glittered in the sunshine.

"Oh, the pretty silver moons!" said the simple soul to himself. And he cautiously approached and picked up one of the "moons."

The next minute he turned as white as rice and sat down on a chair in the shop, still holding the mirror in his hand and looking into it.

"Why, Father," he said, "how did you come here? You are not dead, then? Now the dear gods be praised for that! Yet I could have sworn——But no matter, since you are here alive and well. You are somewhat pale still, but how young you look. You move your lips, Father, and seem to speak, but I do not hear you. You'll come home with me, dear, and live with us just as you used to do? You smile, you smile, that is well."

"Fine mirrors, my young gentleman," said the shopkeeper, "the best that can be made, and that's one of the best of the lot you have there. I see you are a judge."

The young man clutched his mirror tight and sat staring stupidly. Why, here was his father, right in his hand. He trembled. "How much?" he whispered. "Is it for sale?"

"For sale, it is, indeed, most notable sir," said the shopkeeper, "and the price is a trifle, only two *bu*. Such a bargain."

"Two *bu*—only two *bu*! Now the gods be praised for this their mercy!" cried the happy young man. He smiled from ear to ear, and he had the purse out of his bags, and the money out of his purse, in a twinkling.

Now the shopkeeper wished he had asked three *bu* or even five. All the same, he packed the mirror in a fine white box and tied it up with green cords.

"Father," said the young man, when he was back on the street,

28

"before we set out for home we must buy some gifts for my wife."

Now, for the life of him, he could not have told why, but when he came to his home the young man never said a word to Mistress Tassel about buying his old father for two *bu* in the Kyoto shop. That was where he made his mistake, as things turned out.

She was as pleased as could be with her coral hairpins, and her fine new *obi* from Kyoto. "And I'm glad to see him so well and so happy," she said to herself, "but I must say he's been mighty quick to get over his sorrow after all. But men are just like children."

As for her husband, unbeknown to her he took a bit of green silk from her treasure box and spread it in the cupboard. There he placed the mirror in its box of white wood.

Every morning early and every evening late, he went to the cupboard and spoke with his father. Many a jolly talk they had and many a hearty laugh together, and the son was the happiest young man of all that countryside, for he was a simple soul.

But Mistress Tassel had a quick eye and a sharp ear, and it was not long before she noticed her husband's new ways.

"Why does he go so often to the cupboard," she asked herself, "and what has he got there? I should be glad enough to know." Not being one to suffer much in silence, she very soon asked her husband these same questions.

He told her the truth, the good young man. "And now I have my dear old father home again, I'm as happy as the day is long," he said.

"H'm," she said.

"And wasn't two *bu* cheap," he asked, "and wasn't it a strange thing altogether?"

"Cheap, indeed," she said, "and quite strange. And why, if I may ask," she said, "did you say nothing of all this when you first came home?"

The young man grew red. "Indeed, then, I cannot tell you, my dear," he said. "I'm sorry, but I don't know," and with that he went out to his work in the rice fields.

 29

Up jumped Mistress Tassel the minute his back was turned, and to the cupboard she flew on the wings of the wind and flung open the doors with a clang.

"My green silk!" she cried at once, "but I don't see any old father here, only a white wooden box. What can he keep in it?"

She quickly opened the box.

"What an odd flat shining thing!" she said, and taking up the mirror, she looked into it.

For a moment she said nothing at all, but then great tears of anger and jealousy filled her pretty eyes, and her face flushed from forehead to chin.

"A woman," she cried. "A woman! So that is his secret! He keeps a woman in this cupboard. A woman, very young and very pretty—no, not pretty at all, but she thinks herself so. A dancing girl from Kyoto, I'll bet; ill-tempered too—her face is scarlet; and oh, how she frowns, nasty little spitfire. Ah, who could have thought it of him? Ah, it's a miserable girl I am—and I've cooked his dinner and mended his clothes a hundred times. Oh! oh! oh!"

With that, she threw the mirror into its case and slammed the cupboard door closed. She flung herself upon the floor, and cried and sobbed as if her heart would break.

In came her husband.

"I've broken the thong of my sandal," he said, "and I've come to——But what in the world?" and in an instant he was down on his knees beside Mistress Tassel doing what he could to comfort her, and to get her face up from the floor.

"Why, what is it, my own darling?" he asked.

"*Your* own darling!" she answered very fiercely through her sobs. "I want to go home," she cried.

"But, my sweet, you are home, and with your own husband."

"Some husband!" she said, "and some goings-on, with a woman in the cupboard! A hateful, ugly woman that thinks herself beautiful. And she has *my* green silk there with her to boot."

31

"Now, what's all this about women and silk? Certainly you wouldn't begrudge poor old father that little green rag for his bed? Come, my dear, I'll buy you twenty pieces of silk."

At that she jumped to her feet and fairly danced with rage. "Old father! old father! old father!" she screamed. "Am I a fool or a child? I saw the woman with my own eyes."

The poor young man didn't know whether he was on his head or his heels. "Is it possible that my father is gone?" he asked. He took the mirror from the cupboard.

"Oh, good. Still the same old father that I bought for two *bu*. You seem worried, Father; no, then, smile as I do. There, that's better."

Mistress Tassel came like a little fury and snatched the mirror from his hand. She gave only one look into it and hurled it to the other end of the room. It made such a clang against the woodwork that servants and neighbors came rushing in to see what was the matter.

"It is my father," said the young man. "I bought him in Kyoto for two *bu*."

"He keeps a woman in the cupboard who has stolen my green silk," sobbed the wife.

After this there was a great to-do. Some of the neighbors took the man's part and some the woman's, with such a clatter and chatter and noise as never was; but they could not settle the matter, and none of them would look into the mirror, because they said it was bewitched.

They might have gone on the way they were until doomsday, but one of them finally said, "Let us ask the Lady Abbess, for she is a wise woman." And off they all went.

The Lady Abbess was a pious woman, the head of a convent of nuns. She was holy in her prayers and meditations and she was clever, too, at human affairs. They took the mirror to her. She held it in her hands and looked into it for a long time.

At last she spoke. "This poor woman," she said, touching the mirror, "for it's as plain as daylight that it is a woman—this poor woman was so troubled in her mind at the disturbance that she

caused in a quiet house, that she has taken vows, shaved her head, and become a holy nun. Thus she is in her right place here. I will keep her, and instruct her in prayers and meditations. Go home, my children. Forgive and forget, be friends."

Then all the people said, "The Lady Abbess is a wise woman." And she kept the mirror with her treasures.

Mistress Tassel and her husband went home hand in hand.

"So I was right, you see, after all," she said.

"Yes, yes, my dear," said the simple young man, "of course. But I am wondering how my old father will like living at the holy convent. He was never much of a one for religion."

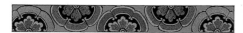 33

The Magic Teakettle

LONG ago, in the temple of Morinji, there lived an old priest who was very holy.

Now, there were three things about this reverend man. First he spent most of his time in meditation and prayers and knew many strange and mystical things. Second, he had exquisite taste, and nothing pleased him so much as the ancient tea ceremony of the *Cha-no-yu*. And third, he loved a bargain.

One day he happened upon an ancient teakettle, lying rusty and dirty and half-forgotten in a corner of a poor shop in a back street of his town.

"An ugly bit of old metal," said the holy man to the shopkeeper, "but it will do well enough to boil my humble drop of water for tea. I'll give you three *rin* for it." This he did and took the kettle home, rejoicing; for it was of bronze, fine work, the very thing for the *Cha-no-yu*.

A young priest cleaned and scoured the teakettle, and it came out as pretty as you please. The old priest turned it this way and that, and upside down, looked into it, tapped it with his fingernail. He smiled. "A bargain," he cried, "a bargain," and rubbed his hands. He placed the kettle upon a box covered with a purple cloth, and sat down to admire it. Soon his head dropped forward and he slept.

And then, a wonderful thing happened. The teakettle moved,

though no hand was near it. A hairy head, with two bright eyes, looked out of the spout. The lid jumped up and down. Four brown and hairy paws appeared, and a fine bushy tail. In a minute the kettle jumped down from the box and pranced round and round looking at things.

"A very comfortable room, to be sure," said the teakettle.

Pleased enough to find itself in such a fine home, it soon began to dance and to sing at the top of its voice. Three or four young priests were studying in the next room. "The old man is lively," they said. "What can he be up to?" And they laughed.

Oh my, the noise that the teakettle made! Bang! bang! Thud! thud! thud!

The young priests soon stopped laughing. One of them slid open the door and peeped through.

"Arah, the devil and all's in it!" he cried. "Here's the master's old teakettle turned into a sort of a badger. The gods protect us from witchcraft, or for certain we shall be lost!"

"And I scoured it just an hour ago," said another young priest, and he fell to his knees to pray.

A third laughed. "I'm for a nearer view of the hobgoblin," he said.

So they left their books in a twinkling, and started chasing the teakettle to catch it. But could they catch that teakettle? Not a bit of it. It danced and it leaped and it flew up into the air. The priests rushed here and there, slipping upon the floor. They grew hot. They grew breathless.

"Ha, ha! Ha, ha!" laughed the teakettle. "Catch me if you can!" laughed the wonderful teakettle.

Soon the old priest awoke.

"And what's the meaning of this racket," he said, "disturbing me at my holy meditations and all?"

"Master, master," cried the young priests, panting and mopping their brows, "your teakettle is bewitched. It was a badger, no less. And the dance it has been giving us, you'd never believe!"

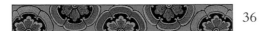 36

"Stuff and nonsense," said the old priest. "Bewitched? Not a bit of it. There it sits on its box, just where I put it."

Sure enough, so it did, looking as hard and cold and innocent as you please. There was not a hair of a badger near it. It was the young priests who looked foolish.

"A likely story indeed," said the priest. "A kettle that turned into a badger—no, no! Go back to your books, my sons, and pray to be preserved from the perils of illusion."

That very night the holy man filled the kettle with water from the spring and set it on the *hibachi* to boil for his cup of tea. When the water began to boil—

"Ai! Ai!" the kettle cried. "Help! I'm burning!" And it hopped off the fire as quick as you please.

"Sorcery!" cried the priest. "Black magic! A devil! A devil! A devil! Mercy on me! Help! Help! Help!" He was frightened out of his wits, the dear good man. All the young priests came running to see what was the matter.

"The teakettle is bewitched," he gasped. "It was a badger, assuredly it was a badger . . . it both speaks and leaps about the room."

"No, master," said one of the young priests. "See how it rests upon its box."

And sure enough, so it did.

"Most reverend sir," said the young priests, "let us all pray to be preserved from the perils of illusion."

The very next day, the priest sold the teakettle to a tinker for twenty copper coins.

"It's a mighty fine bit of bronze," said the priest. "Mind, I'm giving it away to you, I'm sure I cannot tell what for." Ah, he was the one for a bargain! The tinker was a happy man and carried the kettle home. He turned it this way and that, and upside down, and looked into it.

"A pretty piece," said the tinker, "a very good bargain." And

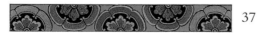 37

when he went to bed that night he put the kettle beside him, to see it first thing in the morning.

He awoke at midnight and looked at the kettle by the bright light of the moon.

Presently it moved, although there was no hand near it.

"Strange," said the tinker, but he was a man who took things as they came.

A hairy head, with two bright eyes, looked out of the kettle's spout. The lid jumped up and down. Four brown and hairy paws appeared, and a fine bushy tail. It came quite close to the tinker and laid a paw upon him.

"Well?" said the tinker.

"I am not wicked," said the teakettle.

"No," said the tinker.

"But I like to be well treated. I am a badger teakettle."

"So it seems," said the tinker.

"At the temple they called me names, and beat me and set me on the fire. I couldn't stand it, you know."

"I like your spirit," said the tinker.

"I think I shall settle down with you," said the kettle.

"Shall I keep you in a lacquer box?" asked the tinker.

"Not a bit of it, keep me with you; let us have a talk now and again. I am very fond of a pipe. I like rice to eat, and beans and sweet things."

"A cup of *saké* sometimes?" asked the tinker.

"Well, yes, now that you mention it."

"I'm willing," said the tinker.

"Thank you kindly," said the teakettle, "and, as a beginning, would you object to my sharing your bed? The night has turned a little chilly."

"Not the least in the world," said the tinker.

The tinker and the teakettle became the best of friends. They ate

and talked together. The kettle knew about many things and was very good company.

One day the kettle asked, "Are you poor?"

"Yes," said the tinker, "quite poor."

"Well, I have a happy thought. For a teakettle, I am unusual—really very talented."

"I believe you," said the tinker.

"My name is *Bumbuku-Chagama*. I am the very prince of Badger Teakettles."

"How do you do, my lord," said the tinker.

"If you'll take my advice," said the teakettle, "you'll build a little theater and carry me around as a show. I really am unusual, and it's my opinion you'd make a mint of money."

"That would be hard work for you, my dear *Bumbuku*."

"Not at all. Let us start immediately," said the teakettle.

So they did. The tinker bought scenery and made a portable theater, and he called the show *Bumbuku-Chagama*. How the people flocked to see the fun! For the wonderful and most talented teakettle danced and sang, and walked the tightrope. It played such tricks and had such funny ways that the people laughed until their sides ached. It was a treat to see the teakettle bow as gracefully as a lord and thank the people for their patience.

The *Bumbuku-Chagama* was the talk of the countryside, and people came from far and wide to see the badger teakettle perform. As for the tinker, he was happy just to collect the money and he grew fat and rich. He even went to the Royal Palace, where the princesses and great ladies made much of the wonderful teakettle.

After many years, the tinker retired from business, and the teakettle came to him with tears in its bright eyes.

"I'm much afraid it's time to leave you," it said.

"Now, don't say that, *Bumbuku*, dear," said the tinker. "We'll be so happy together now that we are rich."

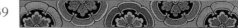

"I've come to the end of my time," said the teakettle. "You'll not see old *Bumbuku* any more. From now on I shall be an ordinary kettle, nothing more or less."

"Oh, my dear *Bumbuku*, what shall I do?" cried the poor tinker in tears.

"I think I would like to be given to the temple of Morinji, as a very sacred treasure," said the teakettle.

It never spoke or moved again. So the tinker presented it as a very sacred treasure to the temple, and gave half of his wealth along with it.

And the teakettle was held in wondrous esteem for many years.

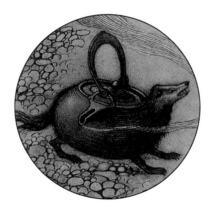

 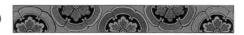

Hana-Saka-Jiji

IN the early days there lived a good old couple. They were honest and hardworking, but they had always been poor. Now in their old age it was all they could do to make both ends meet, the poor old people.

But they did not complain, not a bit. They were as cheerful as the day is long. If they ever went to bed cold or hungry they said nothing about it, and if they had any food in the house you can be sure they shared it with their dog, Shiro, for they loved him dearly. He was faithful, good, and clever.

One evening while the old man and the old woman were digging in their garden, Shiro began to sniff and scratch up the earth with his paws.

"What can the dog be getting into now?" asked the old woman.

"Oh, nothing at all," replied the old man. "He's playing."

"It's more than playing," said the old woman. "I think he's found something."

The dog had dug a pretty big hole by this time, and he went on scratching with his paws for dear life and barking short and sharp. The old man helped dig with his shovel, and before long they uncovered a big box of hidden treasure—silver and gold, jewels and other riches.

The good old couple were overjoyed. They praised their clever dog, and he jumped up and licked their faces. Then they carried the treasure into the house. The dog ran to and fro and barked.

Now, next door to the good old couple lived another old couple, who were always envious and discontented. They had been peeping through a hole in the bamboo hedge and saw Shiro find the hidden treasure. They were so angry and envious that they could think of nothing else.

At last the bad old man came to the good old man.

"I've come to ask for the loan of your dog," he said.

"With all my heart," said the good old man. "Take him and welcome."

So the bad old man brought Shiro home. And the bad old man and his wife put a supper, of all kinds of fine things to eat, before the dog.

"Honorable Dog," they said, "you are good and wise. Eat and afterward find us treasure."

But the dog would not eat.

"All the more left for us," said the greedy old couple, and they ate the dog's supper in a twinkling. Then they tied a string around his neck and dragged him into the garden to find treasure. But not a bit of treasure did he find, nor a glint of gold, nor a shred of rich fabric.

"The devil's in the beast," cried the bad old man, and he beat the dog with a big stick. Then Shiro began to scratch up the earth with his paws.

"Oho! Oho!" said the bad old man to his wife. "Now for the treasure."

But it was not treasure that the dog dug up. No, it was a heap of rubbish, and it smelled so disgusting that the bad old couple had to run away, hiding their noses in their sleeves.

"Arah, arah!" they cried. "The dog has deceived us." And that very night they killed poor Shiro and buried him in the woods at the foot of a tall pine tree.

When the good old man and the good old woman heard the dog

was gone, they wept bitter tears. They picked flowers for the poor dog's grave and burned incense to comfort the poor dog's spirit.

Then, in memory of his dear Shiro, the good old man cut down the pine tree, and made a large bowl from its wood. "When we grind our rice in this bowl each day, we will think of Shiro," he said to his wife. Then he put some rice in the bowl and pounded it.

"Wonder of wonders," cried the old woman, who was watching. "Good man, our rice has all turned into broad gold pieces!"

So it had.

The bad old man soon arrived to ask for the loan of the bowl.

"Take it," said the good old man, who was always kind. "I'm sure you're welcome."

When the bad old man got home he quickly filled the bowl with rice. And he pounded away at it for dear life's sake.

"Do you see any gold coming?" he asked his wife, who was watching.

"Not a bit," she said, "but the rice looks strange."

And strange it was, mildewed and rotten, of no use to man or beast.

"Arah, arah!" they cried. "The magic bowl has deceived us." And in their fury they lit a fire and burned the bowl.

"I've come for my bowl," said the good old man the next day.

"It's gone. It fell into the fire," said his neighbor. The good old man said nothing, but he took some of the ashes of the bowl as a remembrance of his dear dog.

Now it was midwinter, and all the trees were bare. There was not a flower or a leaf to be seen.

As the good old man was walking home with the ashes, a gust of wind scattered some of them over the empty branches of a cherry tree. In a moment the tree was covered with blossoms.

"I've made a dead tree bloom!" cried the good old man. Word of the miracle quickly spread through the village and the Prince invited the good old man to his palace.

43

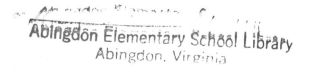

He knocked at the palace gate and said, "I am *Hana-saka-jiji*, the man who makes dead trees blossom."

The Prince was amazed when he saw his cherry trees and his peach trees and his plum trees magically blossom.

"Why," he said, "it is midwinter, and we have the joys of spring." And he called his wife and her maidens and all his own servants to see the work of *Hana-saka-jiji*. At last he sent the old man home with a rich reward.

Now what of the bad old couple? Were they content to let things be? Oh no.

They gathered together all the ashes that were left, and when they had put them in a basket they went about the town crying:

"We are the *Hana-saka-jiji*. We can make dead trees blossom."

The Prince and all his company came out to see the show. And the bad old man climbed up into a tree and scattered his ashes.

But the tree never blossomed, not one bit. The ashes flew into the Prince's eyes, and the Prince flew into a rage. What a commotion! The bad old couple were caught and beaten. Sad and sorry they crept home that night. It is hoped that they mended their ways. In any case, the good people, their neighbors, grew rich and lived happily all their days.

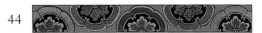

The Cold Lady

ONCE an old man and a young man left their village together and set off on a journey to a distant province. When they had finished their business they turned their faces homeward. It was the start of the winter season, which everyone knows is an evil time for wayfarers.

Now as they journeyed, they became lost, and, being in a lonely part of the country, they wandered all day long and came upon no one to guide them. Near nightfall they found themselves on the bank of a broad and swift-flowing river. There was no bridge and no ferry. Night brought pitch-black clouds and a brisk wind that blew the dry and scanty reeds. Snowflakes began to fall upon the dark water of the river.

"How white, how white they are!" cried the young man.

But the old man shivered. It was bitter cold, and they were in trouble. Tired out, the old man sat down on the ground. He drew his cloak around him and clasped his hands about his knees. The young man blew on his fingers to warm them. He went up the bank a little, and at last he found a small deserted hut.

"It's not much," said the young man, "but any shelter is better than none on such a night." So he carried his companion into the hut. They had no food and no fire, but there was a bundle of dried leaves in the corner. Here they lay down and covered themselves with their straw raincoats. And, in spite of the cold, they soon fell asleep.

About midnight the young man was awakened by an icy chill on his cheek. The door of the hut stood wide open, and he could see the whirling snowstorm outside. It was not very dark. "Curse the wind!" said the young man. "It has blown open the door, and the snow has drifted in and covered my feet," and he raised himself upon his elbow. Then he saw that there was a woman in the hut.

She knelt by his friend the old man, and bent low over him until their faces almost met. Her face was white and beautiful. Her trailing garments were white. Her hair was white with the snow that had fallen upon it. Her hands were stretched over the man who slept, and bright icicles hung from her fingertips. Her breath came from her parted lips like white smoke. Soon she rose up very tall and slender. Snow fell from her in a shower as she moved.

"That was easy," she murmured, and came to the young man. Sinking down beside him she took his hand in hers. If the young man was cold before, he was colder now. He grew numb from head to heel. It felt to him as if his very blood froze, and his heart was a lump of ice that stood still in his chest. A deathly sleep stole over him.

This is my death, he thought. Can this be all? Thank the gods there is no pain.

But then the Cold Lady spoke. "It is only a boy," she said. "A pretty boy," she said, stroking his hair. "I cannot kill him."

"Listen," she said. The young man moaned.

"You must never speak of me, nor of this night," she said. "Not to father, nor mother, nor sister, nor brother, nor to wedded wife, nor to boy child, nor to girl child, nor to sun, nor moon, nor water, fire, wind, rain, snow. Now swear it."

He swore it. "Fire—wind—rain—snow . . ." he murmured, and fell into a deep sleep.

When he awoke it was high noon and the warm sun was shining. A kind countryman held him in his arms and made him drink from a steaming cup.

"Now, boy," said the countryman, "you should be fine. By the

mercy of the gods I came in time, though what brought me to this hut, a good three *ri* out of my way, the gods alone know. As for the good old man, your companion, it is a different matter. He is past help."

"Alack!" cried the young man. "Alack, for the snow and the storm, and the bitter, bitter night! My friend is dead."

But he said no more then, nor did he when a day's journey brought him home to his own village. For he remembered his oath. And the Cold Lady's words were in his ear.

"You must never speak of me, nor of this night. Not to father, nor mother, nor sister, nor brother, nor to wedded wife, nor to boy child, nor to girl child, nor to sun, nor moon, nor water, fire, wind, rain, snow. . . ."

Some years later, in the leafy summertime, the young man took another long journey. As he was returning home, about sundown, he noticed a girl walking in the path a little way ahead of him. It seemed as though she had come some distance, for she wore sandals on her feet and she carried a bundle. She drooped and walked wearily. When the young man caught up with her he saw at once that the girl was very young and fair.

"Young maiden," he said, "where are you going?"

"Sir," she replied, "I am bound for Yedo, where I intend to find work as a servant. I have a sister there who will find me a position."

"What is your name?" he asked.

"My name is O'Yuki."

"O'Yuki," said the young man, "you look very pale."

"Alas, sir," she murmured, "I faint with the heat of this summer day." And as she stood in the path her slender body swayed, and she slid to his feet in a swoon.

The young man lifted her gently, and carried her in his arms to his mother's house. As he looked at her face, he shivered slightly.

"Well," he said to himself, "these summer days turn chilly about sundown, or so it seems to me."

When O'Yuki awoke, she thanked the young man and his mother sweetly for their kindness. Since she had little strength to continue her journey, they invited her to spend the night in their house. As it turned out, she stayed there for many nights and never continued on to Yedo, for the young man grew to love her, and made her his wife before many months had passed. Daily she became more beautiful. Her little hands, no matter how much she used them for work in the house and work in the fields, were as white as jasmine flowers. The hot sun could not burn her neck, or her pale and delicate cheek.

Over the years she had seven children, all as fair as she, and they grew up tall and strong with straight noble limbs. Their equal could not be found in that countryside. Their mother loved them dearly, and cared for them joyously and worked hard for them. In spite of the passing years, in spite of the joys and cares of motherhood, she looked like a young maiden and never seemed to age. She had no wrinkles, no dimness to her eyes, and no gray hairs.

All the women of the village marveled at these things, and gossiped about her endlessly. But O'Yuki's husband was the happiest man for miles round, what with his fair wife and his lovely children.

One winter evening, O'Yuki, after putting her children to bed and warmly covering them, sat with her husband in the next room. The charcoal glowed in the *hibachi*. All the doors of the house were closely shut, for it was bitter cold, and outside the first big flakes of a snowstorm had begun to fall. O'Yuki stitched diligently at little bright-colored garments. A candle stood on the floor beside her, and its light fell full upon her face.

Her husband looked at her, musing. . . .

"Dear," he said, "when I look at you tonight I am reminded of something strange that happened to me many years ago."

O'Yuki spoke not at all, but stitched diligently.

"It was an adventure or a dream," said her husband, "and which it was I cannot tell. Strange it was, as a dream, yet I think I did not sleep."

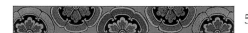

O'Yuki went on sewing.

"Then, only then, I saw a woman, who was as beautiful as you are and as white . . . indeed, she was very like you."

"Tell me about her," said O'Yuki, not lifting her eyes from her work.

"Why," said the man, "I have never spoken of her to anybody." Yet he spoke then, to his misfortune. He told of his journey, and how he and his companion, being lost in a snowstorm, took shelter in a hut. He spoke of the white Cold Lady, and of how his friend had died in her chilly embrace.

"Then she came to my side and leaned over me, but she said, 'It is only a boy . . . a pretty boy . . . I cannot kill him.' How cold she was . . . how cold. . . . Afterward she made me swear, before she left me she made me swear. . . ."

"You must never speak of me, nor of this night," O'Yuki said. "Not to father, nor mother, nor brother, nor sister, nor to wedded wife, nor to boy child, nor to girl child, nor to sun, nor moon, nor water, fire, wind, rain, snow. All this you swore to me, my husband, yes, to me. And after all these years you have broken your oath. Unkind, unfaithful, and untrue!" She folded her work and laid it aside. Then she went to where the children were, and bent her face over each in turn.

The eldest murmured "Cold . . . Cold . . ." so she drew up the quilt over his shoulder.

The youngest cried, "Mother" and threw out his little arms.

She said, "I have grown too cold to weep any more."

With that she came back to her husband. "Farewell," she said. "Even now I cannot kill you, for my little children's sakes. Guard them well."

The man lifted up his eyes and saw her. Her face was white and beautiful. Her trailing garments were white. Her hair was white as if snow had fallen upon it. Her breath came from her parted lips like white smoke.

51

"Farewell! Farewell!" she cried, and her voice grew thin and chilled like a piercing winter wind. Her form grew vague as a snow wreath or a white vaporous cloud. For an instant it hung upon the air. Then it rose up through the smoke hole in the ceiling and was seen no more.

 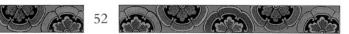

Who Shall Marry the Rat's Daughter?

IN the village where he lived, Mr. Nedzumi, the rat, was an important fellow—at least he and his wife thought so. They had a good life. Their home had for generations been located on a snug, warm, and cozy bank, close to one of the most abundant rice fields in the countryside. There the crops never failed. In spring they could nibble their fill of the young green shoots and in autumn they could stock their storeroom with enough grain to last all through the coming winter.

Mr. and Mrs. Rat had just one daughter, whose beauty was unsurpassed in the whole province. She was completely white and was named Yuki, because of her resemblance to pure snow.

It is little wonder, then, that as she grew up more and more beautiful and intelligent and graceful, her father's ambitions for her grew, too, and he decided to marry her to the most important being in the land.

Now, Mr. Rat's village was located not far from a famous temple, and Mr. Rat sometimes consulted the wise old priest when he had a problem. The priest was well aware of Mr. Rat's self-importance and his little weaknesses, and had in vain tried to teach him the virtues of humility.

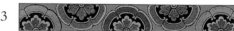

One summer morning Mr. Rat hammered on the gong at the temple door. I'm sure the priest can advise me on the best way to find a suitable husband for my daughter, he thought.

"Welcome, Mr. Rat. What can I do for you today?" said the old priest, for he knew from experience that the rat seldom showed up at the temple unless he had a request to make.

Mr. Rat told the priest what was on his mind—that he wanted only the finest marriage for his daughter, and didn't know how to obtain it.

"That is a difficult question," said the priest, "and it will require much thought. Come back in three days." When Mr. Rat returned on the third day, the old priest gave this answer: "There is no doubt that apart from the gods there is no one so powerful as His Majesty the Sun. If I had a daughter, and wished the best marriage for her, I would speak with the Sun. Approach him when he comes down to our earth at sundown, for then he is clothed in his most gorgeous garments. Besides, he is more easily approached when his day's work is done and he is about to take his well-earned rest. If I were you I would lose no time, but go to him this very evening with your honorable wife and daughter."

"A thousand thanks," said Mr. Rat. "No time is to be lost if I am to get my family together at the time and place you mention."

"Good luck to you," said the priest. "May I greet you the next time I see you as father-in-law to His Majesty the Sun."

That evening Mr. and Mrs. Rat and their daughter put on their finest clothes, and as the sun came earthward and his rays illuminated the gloom under the great pines, Mr. Rat, not the least bit shy, made his request.

His Majesty replied, "I am extremely honored by your kind intention of allowing me to wed your beautiful daughter, O Yuki San, but may I ask your reason for selecting me to be your son-in-law?"

To this Mr. Rat said, "We wish to marry our daughter to whoever

is the most powerful being in the world, and that is why we desire to offer her to you in marriage."

"Yes," said His Majesty, "I can see why you would imagine me to be the most powerful being in the world, but, unfortunately, it has been my misfortune to discover that there is one other even more powerful than myself, against whom I have no power. It is to him that you should very certainly marry your daughter."

"And who may that be?" said Mr. Rat.

"It is the Cloud," said the Sun. "Often when I try to shine on the world, he comes across my path and covers my face so that my subjects cannot see me. And so long as he does this I am altogether in his power. If, therefore, it is the most powerful being in the world that you seek for your daughter, the honorable O Yuki San, you must marry her to the Cloud."

Both father and mother saw the wisdom of the Sun's advice, and they set off immediately to speak with the Cloud.

The Cloud said, "I am indeed honored by your proposal that I marry your beautiful daughter. It is quite true, as His Majesty the Sun says, that I have the strength to overpower him, but I am not the most powerful being in the world, for there is another who is more powerful than I."

"You surprise me," said Mr. Rat. "And who would that be?"

"It is the Wind," said the Cloud. "The Wind can easily blow me from my spot in the sky. Why don't you go down to the seashore and await his coming. He will surely be there soon."

"Many thanks." said Mr. Rat, and off they went.

The Wind came toward them, rippling the face of the water with smiles. "Mr. Cloud is a flatterer," said the Wind to Mr. Rat. "But to call me the most powerful being in the world is nonsense. Now tell me, where do you come from? Why, in that very village there is one stronger than I—namely, the high wall that fences in the house of your good neighbor. If your daughter must marry the strongest and most powerful thing in the world, you must wed her to the wall."

 55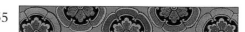

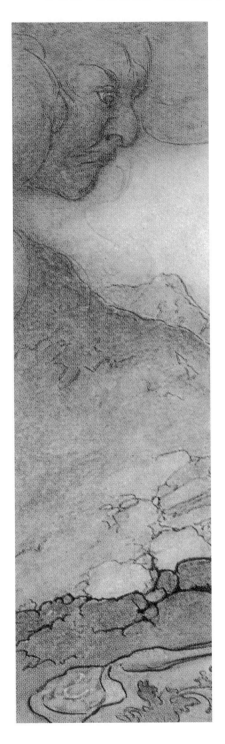

By this time the Rat family was getting tired and discouraged by the stress of their long journey and the many disappointments. But Mr. Rat said there was nothing to do but to return home. He knew the wall that the Wind had spoken of, though he had certainly never thought much of it.

So they trudged homeward, and it was a difficult trip, for the Cloud had hidden the Sun, and the Wind had angered the Cloud, who showed his annoyance by tossing down some rain upon them. They approached their home soaked through, bedraggled and all worn out.

"Oh, Great Wall," said Mr. Rat. "You may marry my beautiful and talented daughter. The Wind says you are more powerful than he, for he cannot blow you down no matter how hard he tries."

"I the strongest! The Wind is sorely mistaken. Why, only yesterday a big brown rat, who couldn't be bothered going around me, chewed a hole right through me. The strongest thing in the world! I'm afraid it's not me. The next time the Wind comes this way he'll rush through the hole and tell you that a simple rat is the strongest being in the world!"

At this moment the rain stopped, the clouds rolled by, and the sun shone out, and Mr. and Mrs. Rat went home congratulating themselves that they had finally discovered the truth.

A month later, O Yuki San announced that she was in love with the fine young rat who lived next door. Her parents were delighted to give their blessings to the marriage, for had the simple rat not proved himself to be the most powerful being in the world?

Urashima

URASHIMA was a fisherman of the Inland Sea. Every night, through the long hours of darkness, he fished, catching fishes both great and small. This is how he made his living.

One morning as he was heading home from the sea with his catch, he saw a group of children gathered around a tortoise, poking it and prodding it with a stick and laughing. "Stop that," said Urashima. "Leave the poor tortoise alone!"

"We found him and we can do as we please," said the children.

Urashima reached in his pocket and found a few coins. "Here," he said. "I will buy the tortoise from you."

The children grabbed the money and ran off toward a candy shop. "Now off you go and don't let those children catch you again," said Urashima to the tortoise as it plodded off into the sea and swam away.

That evening Urashima set out in his fishing boat again. The moon shone brightly upon the sea. And Urashima kneeled in his boat and dabbled his right hand in the green water. He leaned low, until his hair was spread upon the waves. He paid no attention to his boat or to his trailing fishing net. Neither awake or asleep, he drifted in his boat until he came to a haunted place.

Then a voice called to him. "Urashima. Urashima." And up from

WARWICK GOBLE

the water rose the Daughter of the Deep Sea. "I have come to thank you for your kindness to the poor tortoise." And she took the fisherman in her arms and sank with him, down, down to the palace of the Dragon God of the Sea. The fisherman Urashima had never seen such riches. The palace was covered with precious stones and beautiful jewels. Coral and gold and silver were everywhere.

"Welcome," said the Dragon God. "Please be our guest for as long as you wish."

"I cannot stay long," said Urashima, "for my wife and children will be worried about me."

Then Urashima was served a great banquet of delicious foods, and a rainbow of fish appeared and performed a wondrous dance for his entertainment.

Three nights quickly passed. "I could stay here forever," said Urashima, "but it is time for me to return to my family and my life above the sea." So the Daughter of the Deep Sea brought him up to the sand and the seashore.

"Are we near your home?" she said.

"Within a stone's throw."

"Take this," she said, "in memory of me." She gave him a box made of mother-of-pearl. It was rainbow-tinted and its clasps were of coral and of jade.

"Do not open it," she said. "Oh, fisherman, do not open it, no matter what." And with that she sank back into the sea.

As for Urashima, he ran beneath the pine trees toward his home. And as he went he laughed for joy. And he tossed up the box to catch the sun.

"Ah, me," he said, "the sweet scent of the pines!" So he went calling to his children with a call that he had taught them, like a sea bird's note. Soon he said, "Are they still asleep? It is strange they do not answer me."

When he came to his house he found four lonely walls on which moss had grown. Nightshade flourished on the threshold, death lilies by the hearth. No living soul was there.

"Now what is this?" cried Urashima. "Have I lost my wits? Have I left my eyes in the deep sea?"

He sat down on the grassy floor and thought for a long time. "The dear gods help me!" he said. "Where is my wife, and where are my little children?"

He went to the village, where he knew all the streets and every building was most familiar. And here he saw people walking to and fro, going about their business. But they were all strange to him.

"Good day," they said. "Good day, stranger."

He saw children at play, and often he put his hand beneath their chins to turn their faces up. Alas, he did it all in vain.

"Where are my little children?" he said. "This is too much for me."

When sunset came, his heart was heavy as stone, and he went and stood at the edge of town. As people passed by he pulled them by the sleeve: "Friend," he said, "I beg your pardon, do you know of a fisherman of this village called Urashima?"

And everyone who passed by answered him, "We never heard of such a one."

Night fell.

"I lose sweet hope," said Urashima.

But then an old, old man came by.

"Oh, old, old man," cried the fisherman, "you have lived a long time; have you heard of Urashima? In this village he was born and raised."

The old man replied, "There was one of that name, but, sir, he was drowned years ago. My grandfather could scarce remember him in the time that I was a little boy. Good stranger, it was three hundred years ago."

"He is dead?" asked Urashima.

"No man more dead than he. His sons are dead and their sons are dead. Good evening to you, stranger."

Then Urashima was afraid. But he said, "I must go to the graveyard where the dead lie and see for myself."

When he arrived at the graveyard, he was cold and tired. "How chilly the night wind blows through the grass! The trees shiver and the leaves turn their pale backs to me," he said.

"And here are my sons' graves, and their sons' graves. Three hundred years! How could this be—I was in the sea palace for only three nights. Oh, I am lonely here among the ghosts. . . . Who will comfort me?" he asked.

The night wind sighed and nothing more.

Then he went back to the seashore. "Who will comfort me?" cried Urashima. But the sky was unmoved and the mountainous waves of the sea rolled on.

"Here is the box," he said. "Perhaps it holds the key to this mystery." And he opened it. There rose from the box a faint white smoke that floated away and out to the far horizon.

"I grow very weary," said Urashima. In a moment his hair turned

as white as snow. He trembled, his body shrank, his eyes grew dim. His skin wrinkled, and his teeth fell out. He who had been so young and strong now swayed and tottered where he stood.

"I am three hundred years old," said Urashima.

He tried to shut the lid of the box, but dropped it, saying, "No, the vapor of immortality is gone forever. But what does it matter?"

Then he laid down upon the sand and died.

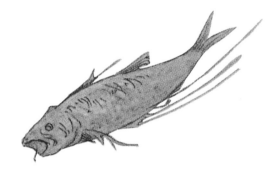

The Girl
With the Black Bowl

LONG ago, in a part of the country not very far from the great city of Kyoto, there lived an honest couple who were as poor as can be. They had one fair daughter. She was as neat and as pretty as a princess, and her manners were very fine. She never complained even though she worked hard outdoors in the rice fields, and indoors she washed and cooked and drew water. She went barefoot and always wore a gray homespun gown; her hair was tied back with a tough wisteria tendril. She was the sweetest young woman who ever made do with a bed of dry moss and no supper.

By and by her father died. Then, within the year, her mother grew very ill. Soon she lay in a corner of the cottage waiting for her end, with her daughter nearby crying bitter tears.

"Child," said the mother, "do you know you are as pretty as a princess?"

"Am I that?" said the girl, and continued with her crying.

"Do you know that your manners are fine?" asked the mother.

"Are they, then?" said the girl, and continued her crying.

"My own baby," said the mother, "could you stop your crying a minute and listen to me?"

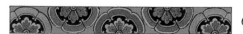 

So the girl stopped crying and put her head close by her mother's on the thin pillow.

"Now listen," said the mother, "and afterward remember. I am dying, and you will be alone in the world. Your great beauty is like a magnet, and I must protect you, for the world is not all good. Fetch me the great black rice bowl from the shelf."

The girl got it.

"See, now, I put it on your head and all your beauty is hidden away."

"Alack, Mother," said the poor girl, "it is heavy."

"Believe me, this is for your own good," said her mother. "If you love me, promise me that you will not remove it until the time comes."

"I promise! I promise! But how shall I know when the time comes?"

"That you shall know. . . ."

The girl with the black bowl upon her head held her mother in her arms. Her mother smiled at her, and then she died.

When all the rice in the pantry was eaten, the girl with the wooden bowl knew that she must starve or go and find more. First she tended her father's and mother's graves and recited many prayers. Then she put on her sandals, tied her few possessions in a blue printed scarf, and set out all alone to seek her fortune. She was a brave girl!

Despite her slenderness and pretty feet she was an odd sight, and people let her know it. The great black bowl covered her head and shadowed her face. As she went through a village two women looked up from washing their clothes in the stream; they stared and laughed.

"It's an evil spirit come alive," said one.

"Look at her—it is enough to make a person sick," said the other.

On went the poor girl. Sometimes the children pelted her with mud and pebbles for sport. Sometimes she was handled roughly by village louts, who pulled at her dress as she went by; they even

grabbed the bowl itself and tried to pull it from her head by force. But they only played that game once, for the bowl stung them as fiercely as if it were covered with thorns, and the bullies ran away howling.

The girl tried to find work, but no one wanted to hire someone with a black bowl on her head.

At last, one day, she was too weak and tired to go on. She sat down on a stone and began to cry as if her heart would break. Down rolled her tears from under the black bowl.

A wandering ballad-singer was passing by, with his instrument slung across his back. He noticed the tears on the girl's fair chin. It was all he could see of her face. "Oh, girl with the black bowl on your head," he said, "why do you sit weeping by the roadside?"

"I weep," she answered, "because the world is hard. I am hungry and tired. . . . No one will give me work so I can earn money."

"Now that's unfortunate," said the ballad-singer, for he had a kind heart, "but I haven't a *rin* of my own, or it would be yours. Indeed I am sorry for you. In the circumstances the best I can do for you is to make you a little song." With that he whipped his instrument around, strummed on it with his fingers, and began to sing. "To the tears on your fair chin," he said, and sang:

"The white cherry blooms by the roadside,
How black is the canopy of cloud!
The wild cherry droops by the roadside,
Beware of the black canopy of cloud.
Hark, hear the rain, hear the rainfall
From the black canopy of cloud.
Alas, the wild cherry, its sweet flowers are marred,
Marred are the sweet flowers, forlorn on the spray!"

"Sir, I do not understand your song," said the girl with the bowl on her head.

"It is plain enough," said the ballad-singer, and went on his way.

 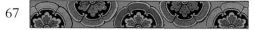

He came to the house of a rich farmer. In he went, and he was asked to sing before the master of the house.

"With all the will in the world," said the ballad-singer. "I will sing him a new song that I have just made." So he sang of the wild cherry and the great black cloud.

When he had finished, the master of the house said, "Tell us the meaning of your song."

"Certainly," said the ballad-singer. "The wild cherry is the face of a maiden whom I saw sitting by the wayside. She wore a great black wooden bowl on her head, which is the great black cloud in my song, and from under it her tears flowed like rain, for I saw the drops on her fair chin. And she said that she wept for hunger, and because no one would give her work or pay her money."

"If only I could help the poor girl with the bowl on her head," said the master of the house.

"That you may if you wish," said the ballad-singer. "She sits but a stone's throw from your gate."

The long and short of it was that the girl was put to work in the rich farmer's harvest fields. All day long she worked in the waving rice, and the sun shone down upon the black bowl. The work was hard and the sun was hot, but she had food to eat and a place to sleep, and she was content.

Her master was pleased with her work and kept her in the fields until the harvest was gathered in. Then he took her into his house, where there was plenty for her to do, for his wife was sickly. Now the girl lived well and happily as a bird, and sang as she went about her chores. And every night she thanked the gods for her good fortune. Still she wore the black bowl upon her head.

The New Year approached. "Bustle, bustle," said the farmer's wife. "Scrub and cook and sew. Put your best foot foremost, my dear, for we must have the house look its very neatest."

"To be sure, and with all my heart," said the girl. "But, mistress, if I may be so bold as to ask, are we having a party?"

"Indeed we are, and many of them," said the farmer's wife. "My son who lives in Kyoto is coming home for a visit."

When the handsome young man arrived home, the neighbors were invited over and there was great merrymaking. They feasted and danced, they joked and sang. Many a bowl of good red rice they ate,

and many a cup of good *saké* they drank. All this time the girl with the bowl on her head worked quietly in the kitchen, well out of the way—the farmer's wife saw to that. All the same, one fine day when the company called for more wine, the son of the house himself took the empty *saké* bottle into the kitchen. What should he see there but the girl sitting upon a pile of firewood and fanning the kitchen fire with a split bamboo fan!

"My life, but I must see what is under that black bowl," said the handsome young man to himself. And sure enough he sought her out every day and peeped as much as he could, which was not very much. But apparently it was enough for him, for he thought no more of the great city of Kyoto, but stayed home to be near the girl with the bowl on her head.

His father laughed and his mother fretted, the neighbors held up their hands, all to no purpose.

"The dear, dear girl with the wooden bowl shall be my bride and no other. I must and will have her," cried the impetuous young man. Very soon he fixed the wedding day himself.

When the time came, the young maidens of the village arrived to dress the bride in a beautiful and costly robe of white brocade, with a train of scarlet silk. On her shoulders they hung a cloak of blue and purple and gold. They chattered, but the bride never said a word. She was sad because she brought her bridegroom nothing, and because his parents were angry at his choice of a wife. She was silent, but the tears glistened on her fair chin.

"Now off with the ugly old bowl," cried the maidens. "It is time to adorn the bride's hair with golden combs." So they tugged at the bowl and would have lifted it away, but they could not move it.

"Try again," they said, and pulled at it with all their might. But it would not stir.

"There's witchcraft in it," they said. "Try a third time." They tried a third time, and still the bowl stuck fast, but it gave out fearsome moans and cries.

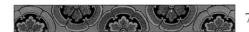 

"Ah! Let be, let be, for pity's sake," said the poor bride, "for you make my head ache."

They were forced to lead her bowl and all to the bridegroom.

"My dear, I am not afraid of the wooden bowl," said the young man.

So they poured the *saké* from the silver flask, and from the silver cup the two of them drank the ceremonial cup of wine that made them man and wife.

Then the black bowl burst asunder with a loud noise, and fell to the ground in a thousand pieces. With it fell a shower of silver and gold, pearls and rubies and emeralds. Great was the astonishment of the guests as they gazed upon a dowry that even for a princess would have been rich and rare.

But the bridegroom looked with love into the bride's face. "My dear," he said, "there are no jewels that shine like your eyes."

71
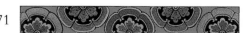

The Sword of Idé

IDÉ the *samurai* was married to a beautiful woman. They had one child, a boy named Fugiwaka. Idé was a mighty man of war, and was often away from home. So the child Fugiwaka was reared by his mother and by his faithful nurse, Matsu, which means "the Pine Tree." And like the pine tree, she was strong and evergreen, unchanging and enduring.

In the house of Idé there was a precious sword. In one battle, an ancestor of Idé's had slain forty-eight of his enemies with this sword. It was Idé's most sacred treasure. He kept it in a safe place with his household gods.

Every morning and evening Fugiwaka came to pray before the household gods, and to pay his respect to the glorious memory of his ancestors. And Matsu, the nurse, knelt by his side.

Every morning and evening, Fugiwaka said, "Show me the sword, O Matsu, my nurse."

And O Matsu answered, "Certainly, my lord. I will show it to you."

Then she brought out the sword and drew off the covering of red and gold brocade. She took the sword from its golden sheath and displayed the bright steel to Fugiwaka. And the child bowed deeply until his forehead touched the mats on the floor.

Every night at bedtime O Matsu sang him songs and lullabies. Then she said, "Will you sleep now, my lord Fugiwaka?"

And the child answered, "I will sleep now, O Matsu."

"Listen, my lord," she said, "and, sleeping or waking, remember. The sword is your treasure. The sword is your trust. The sword is your fortune. Cherish it, guard it, keep it."

"Sleeping or waking, I will remember," said Fugiwaka.

One terrible day Fugiwaka's mother fell sick and died. There was great mourning in the house of Idé. But after a few years, the *samurai* took another bride, and they soon had a son, whom they called Goro. Not long after this Idé himself was slain in an ambush, and his soldiers brought his body home and buried him in the graveyard with his ancestors.

Fugiwaka was now the head of the House of Idé. But the Lady Sadako, his stepmother, was not pleased. Black mischief stirred in her heart. She furrowed her brows and she brooded as she went about her daily chores, carrying her baby in her arms. At night she tossed upon her bed.

"My child is a beggar," she said. "Fugiwaka is the head of the House of Idé. May evil fortune befall him! It is too much," said the proud lady. "I will not allow it—my child a beggar! I would rather strangle him with my hands. . . ." Thus she spoke and tossed upon her bed, thinking of a plan.

When Fugiwaka was fifteen years old Lady Sadako threw him out of the house with only a poor garment upon his back, barefooted, with neither a bite to eat nor a gold piece to see him on his way.

"Ah, Lady Mother," he said, "you treat me wrongly. Why do you banish me from my own home?"

"You are no longer welcome here," she said. "Go, make your own fortune if you can. Your brother Goro is now the head of the House of Idé."

With that she shut the door in his face.

Fugiwaka departed sorrowfully. Down the road he met O Matsu, his nurse. She was dressed for a journey: she had a walking stick in her hand and sandals on her feet.

"My lord," she said, "I have come to follow you to the world's end." Then Fugiwaka wept and knelt before O Matsu.

"Ah," he said, "my nurse, my nurse! And what of my father's sword? I have lost the precious sword of Idé. The sword is my treasure, the sword is my trust, the sword is my fortune. I have promised to cherish it, to guard it, to keep it. But now I have lost it. Woe is me! This is the end of me and the end of the House of Idé!"

"Oh, do not say such things, my lord," said O Matsu. "Here is some gold; you go along and I will return and guard the sword of Idé."

So Fugiwaka continued on with the gold pieces that his nurse gave him.

As for O Matsu, she went straight home and took the sword from its place beside the household gods. She buried it deep in the ground to hide it until the day came when she could safely bring it to her young lord.

But soon the Lady Sadako became aware that the sacred sword was gone.

"It is the nurse!" she cried. "The nurse has stolen it. . . . Bring her to me."

Then the Lady Sadako's people roughly grabbed O Matsu and brought her before their lady. But for all they could do O Matsu's lips were sealed. She spoke not a word, and the Lady Sadako could not find out where the sword was. She pressed her thin lips together.

"The woman is obstinate," she said. "No matter. I know just the cure for such behavior."

So she locked O Matsu in a dark dungeon and gave her neither food nor drink. Every day the Lady Sadako went to the door of the dark dungeon.

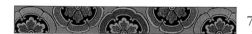
75

"Well," she said, "where is the sword of Idé? Will you tell me?" But O Matsu answered not a word.

Still, she wept and sighed to herself in the darkness—"Alas! Alas! I'll never live to see my young lord again. Yet he must have the sword of Idé, and I shall find a way."

One evening, a week later, the Lady Sadako sat in the garden house to cool herself off, for it was summer. Soon she saw a woman coming toward her through the garden flowers and trees. The woman was frail and slender. As she walked her body swayed and her slow steps faltered.

"Why, this is strange!" said the Lady Sadako. "Here is O Matsu, who was locked in the dark dungeon." And she sat still, watching.

Then O Matsu went to the place where she had buried the sword and scratched at the ground with her fingers. There she was, weeping and moaning and dragging at the earth. The stones cut her hands until they bled. Still she tore away the earth until at last she found the sword. It was in its wrapping of gold and scarlet, and she clasped it tight with a loud cry.

"Woman, I have you now," shrieked the Lady Sadako, "and the sword of Idé as well!" And she leaped from the garden house and ran at full speed. She stretched out her hand to grab O Matsu by the sleeve, but did not catch her or the sword either, for both of them disappeared in a flash, and Lady Sadako clutched nothing—just empty air. Swiftly she rushed to the dungeon, and as she went she called her people to bring torches to light the dark room. There they found the body of poor O Matsu, cold and dead upon the dungeon floor.

"Send me the wise woman," said the Lady Sadako.

So they sent for the wise woman. And the Lady Sadako asked, "How long has she been dead?"

The wise woman said, "She starved to death. She has been dead for two days, the poor good soul."

As for the sword of Idé, it was not found.

 76

That night Fugiwaka tossed to and fro upon his lowly bed in a wayside inn. And it seemed to him that his nurse came to him and knelt by his side. Then he was soothed.

O Matsu said, "Will you sleep now, my lord Fugiwaka?"

And he answered, "I will sleep now, O Matsu."

"Listen, my lord," she said, "and, sleeping or waking, remember. The sword is your treasure. The sword is your trust. The sword is your fortune. Cherish it, guard it, keep it."

The sword was in its wrapping of gold and scarlet, and she laid it at Fugiwaka's side. The boy turned over to sleep, and his hand clasped the sword of Idé.

"Waking or sleeping," he said, "I will remember."

 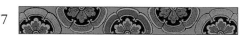

The Tongue-Cut Sparrow

ONCE upon a time there was an old man who lived all alone. Next door an old woman lived all alone. The old man was merry and kind and gentle, with a good word and a smile for all the world. The old woman was sour and sad, as cross a patch as could be found in all the countryside. She grumbled and growled all the time, and never had anything nice to say.

The old man had a pet sparrow that was the apple of his eye. The sparrow could talk and sing and dance and do all kinds of tricks, and was very good company. When the old man came home from work at night, there would be the sparrow twittering on the doorstep. "Welcome home, master," he would say, his head on one side, as pert and pretty as you please. The old man loved him dearly and they were the best of friends.

One day the old man went off to cut wood in the mountains. The old woman was busy at home, for it was her washing day. She made some good starch in a bowl and put it outside her door to cool.

It will be ready when I want to starch my clothes, she said to herself. But that's just where she made a mistake. The little sparrow flew over the bamboo fence and lighted on the edge of the starch

bowl. He pecked at the starch with his little beak. This is delicious, he said to himself, and he pecked and he pecked until all the starch was gone.

Then out came the old woman for the starch to starch her clothes.

Let me tell you, she was angry. She caught the little sparrow roughly in her hand, and, alas and alack! she took a sharp, sharp scissors and cut off his little tongue. "There," she said. "You won't be eating my starch again, you naughty bird!" Then she let him go.

Away flew the poor little sparrow, over hill and over dale.

"And a good riddance, too!" said the old woman.

When the old man came home from the mountains he found his pet sparrow gone. "He ate my starch," said the old woman. "So I cut off his tongue."

"How could you be so cruel," cried the good old man, and he rushed out at once on foot to find his pet, calling, "Sparrow, sparrow, where are you, my tongue-cut sparrow?"

Over hill and over dale he went, calling, "Sparrow, sparrow, where are you, my tongue-cut sparrow?"

At last, in a bamboo grove, he found the sparrow's house, and the sparrow flew out to greet his master. Then there was a great twittering. The sparrow, whose tongue had grown back, called his brothers and sisters and his children and his wife and his mother-in-law and his mother and his grandmother. And they all flew out to honor the kind old man. They brought him into the house and they set him down upon mats of silk. Then they spread a great feast: red rice and vegetables and fish, and who knows what else, and the very best *saké* to drink. The sparrow waited upon the good old man, and his brothers and sisters and his children and his wife and his mother-in-law and his mother and his grandmother helped him.

After supper, the sparrow danced, while his grandmother played music on the *samisen* and the good old man tapped out the rhythm. It was a merry evening.

At last, the old man said, "All good things come to an end. I fear 'tis late and high time I was getting home."

"Not without a little present," said the sparrow.

"Ah, sparrow dear," said the old man, "I'd sooner have yourself than any present. Please come home with me."

But the sparrow shook his head. "I cannot. But I want to give you something in thanks for our fine friendship."

Presently the other sparrows brought in two wicker baskets.

"One of them is heavy," said the sparrow, "and the other is light. Tell me, master, will you take the heavy basket or the light?"

"I'm not so young as I once was," said the good old man. "Thanking you kindly, I'd sooner have the light basket. It will suit me better to carry—that is, if it's all the same to you," he said.

So he went home with the light basket. When he opened it, wonderful to tell, it was full of gold and silver and tortoiseshell and coral and jade and fine rolls of silk. So the good old man would be rich for the rest of his life.

Now, when the bad old woman heard of all this, she was very jealous. "You took the *smaller* basket?" she shouted. And she imagined how many more riches the bigger basket must have contained.

I must have it, she thought, so she put on her sandals and set off. Over hill and over dale she went, and took the road straight to the sparrow's house. There was the sparrow, and there were his brothers and sisters and children and his wife and his mother and his mother-in-law and his grandmother. They were not too pleased to see the bad old woman, but they had fine manners and felt that they couldn't do less than ask her in as she'd come so far. They gave her red rice and white rice and vegetables and fish, and who knows what else, and she gobbled it up in a twinkling, and drank a good cup of *saké*. Then up she got. "I can't waste any more time here," she said, "so you'd best bring out your presents."

They brought in two wicker baskets.

"One of them is heavy," said the sparrow, "and the other is light. Say, mistress, will you take the heavy basket or the light?"

"I'll take the heavy one," said the old woman, quick as a thought. So she heaved it up on her back and off she went. Sure enough it was as heavy as lead.

When she was gone, goodness! how the sparrows did laugh!

No sooner did she reach home than the old woman undid the cords of the basket.

"Now for the gold and silver," she said, and smiled—though she hadn't smiled for a whole year. And she lifted up the lid.

"*Ai! Ai! Kowai! Obaké da! Obaké!*" she screeched.

The basket was full of ugly imps and hobgoblins and demons and devils. Out they came to tease the old woman, to pull her and to poke her, to push her and to pinch her. She had the fright of her life. Off she ran with the creatures chasing behind her, and for all anyone knows, she may be running still.

Momotaro,
Son of the Peach

THERE was once a time when the fairies were not so shy as they are now. That was the time when beasts talked to men, when there were spells and enchantments and magic every day, when there was great store of hidden treasure to be dug up, and adventures for the asking.

At that time, an old man and an old woman lived alone by themselves. They were good people, but they were poor and they had no children.

One fine day, the old woman said, "What are you doing this morning, good man?"

"Oh," said the old man, "I'm off to the mountains to gather twigs for our fire. And what are you doing, good wife?"

"Oh," said the old woman, "I'm off to the stream to wash clothes. It's my washing day," she added.

So the old man went to the mountains and the old woman went to the stream.

Now, while she was washing the clothes, what should she see but a fine ripe peach that came floating down the stream? The peach was big and round, and rosy red on both sides.

"I'm in luck this morning," said the woman, and she pulled the peach to shore with a split bamboo stick.

By and by, when her good man came home from the hills, she set

 83

the peach before him. "Eat, good man," she said. "This is a lucky peach I found in the stream and brought home for you."

But the old man never got a taste of the peach, because all of a sudden the peach burst in two, and inside, where the pit should have been, there was a fine boy baby.

"Mercy me!" said the old woman.

"Mercy me!" said the old man.

The baby boy first ate one half of the peach and then he ate the other half. When he had done this he was finer and stronger than ever.

"Momotaro! Momotaro!" cried the old man, "the eldest son of the peach."

"Truth it is indeed," said the old woman. "He was born in a peach."

Time passed, and the old couple took such good care of Momotaro that he was the strongest and bravest boy of all that countryside. The neighbors nodded their heads and said, "Momotaro is a fine young man!"

"Mother," said Momotaro one day when he was fifteen years old, "pack me some *kimi-dango*" (which is what they called millet dumplings in that village).

"Why do you want *kimi-dango*?" asked his mother.

"Well," said Momotaro, "I'm going on a journey, or as you may say, an adventure, and I shall be needing the *kimi-dango* on the way."

"Where are you going, Momotaro?" asked his mother.

"I'm off to the Ogres' Island," said Momotaro. "The ogres kill our people. I will rid the land of their evil and get their treasure, and I should be obliged if you'd let me have the *kimi-dango* as soon as you can."

So she made him the *kimi-dango*, and he put them in a traveling pack and off he set.

"*Sayonara*, and good luck to you, Momotaro!" cried the old man and the old woman.

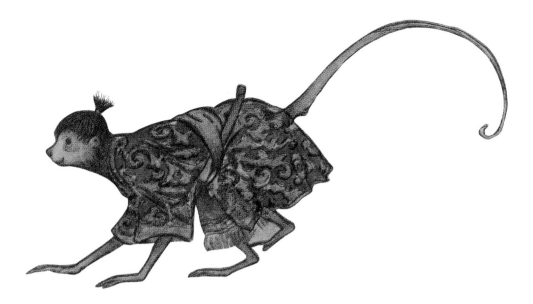

"*Sayonara! Sayonara!*" cried Momotaro.

He hadn't gone far when he met a monkey.

"Kia! Kia!" said the monkey. "Where are you off to, Momotaro?"

"I'm off to the Ogres' Island to have an adventure," replied Momotaro.

"What have you got in your pack?"

"Now you're asking me something," said Momotaro. "Why, I've got some of the best millet dumplings in all Japan."

"Give me one," said the monkey, "and I will go with you."

So Momotaro gave a dumpling to the monkey, and the two of them jogged on together. They hadn't gone far when they met a pheasant.

"Ken! Ken!" said the pheasant. "Tell me, where are you off to, Momotaro?"

"I'm off to the Ogres' Island for an adventure," said Momotaro.

"What have you got in your pack, Momotaro?"

"I've got some of the best dumplings in all Japan."

"Give me one," said the pheasant, "and I will go with you."

So Momotaro gave a millet dumpling to the pheasant, and the three of them jogged on together.

They hadn't gone far when they met a dog.

"Bow! Wow! Wow!" said the dog. "Where are you off to, Momotaro?"

"I'm off to the Ogres' Island."

"What have you got in your pack, Momotaro?"

"I've got some of the best dumplings in all Japan."

"Give me one," said the dog, "and I will go with you."

So Momotaro gave a millet dumpling to the dog, and the four of them jogged on together. By and by they came to the Ogres' Island.

"Now, brothers," said Momotaro, "listen to my plan. The pheasant must fly over the castle gate and peck the ogres. The monkey must climb over the castle wall and pinch the ogres. The dog and I will break the bolts and bars. He will bite the ogres, and I will fight the ogres."

Then there was a great battle.

The pheasant flew over the castle gate: "Ken! Ken! Ken!"

Momotaro broke the bolts and bars, and the dog leaped into the castle courtyard. "Bow! Wow! Wow!"

The brave companions fought until sundown and overcame the ogres. Those that were left alive they took prisoners and tied up with cords—a wicked lot they were.

"Now, brothers," said Momotaro, "let's bring out the ogres' treasure."

So they did.

The treasure was worth having, indeed. There were magic jewels, and caps and coats to make you invisible. There was gold and silver, and jade and coral, and amber and tortoiseshell and mother-of-pearl.

"Here is riches for all," said Momotaro. "Choose, brothers, and take your fill."

"Kia! Kia!" said the monkey. "Thanks, my Lord Momotaro."

"Ken! Ken!" said the pheasant. "Thanks, my Lord Momotaro."

"Bow! Wow! Wow!" said the dog. "Thanks, my dear Lord Momotaro."

Then Momotaro gathered up his share of the treasures and returned home to the old man and the old woman, who welcomed him with joy. Momotaro and the monkey and the dog and the pheasant remained the best of friends and they all lived happily for the rest of their days.

 87

The Matsuyama Mirror

A LONG, long time ago there lived in a quiet village a young man and his wife. They had one child, a little daughter, whom they both loved with all their hearts. I cannot tell you their names, for they have long since been forgotten, but the name of the place where they lived was Matsuyama, in the Province of Echigo.

It happened once, while the little girl was still a baby, that the father had to go to the great city, the capital of Japan, for some business. It was too far for the mother and her little baby to go, so he set out alone, after bidding them good-bye and promising to bring home to them a pretty present.

The mother had never been farther from home than the next village, and she could not help being a little frightened at the thought of her husband taking such a long journey. And yet she was a little proud too, for he was the first man in all that countryside who had been to the big town where the king and his great lords lived, and where there were so many beautiful and unusual things to see.

At last the time came when she thought her husband might be back, so she dressed the baby in her best clothes, and she put on a pretty blue dress that she knew her husband liked.

You may imagine how glad this good wife was to see him come

home safe and sound, and how the little girl clapped her hands and laughed with delight when she saw the pretty toys her father had brought for her. He had much to tell of all the wonderful things he had seen upon the journey and in the town itself.

"I have brought you a very pretty thing," he said to his wife. "It is called a mirror. Look and tell me what you see inside." He gave her a plain white wooden box, in which she found a round piece of metal. One side was white, like frosted silver, and decorated with raised figures of birds and flowers; the other side was as bright as the clearest crystal. Into it the young mother looked with delight and astonishment, for looking back at her, with parted lips and bright eyes, was a smiling happy face.

"What do you see?" asked the husband again, pleased at her astonishment and glad to show that he had learned something while he was away.

"I see a pretty woman looking at me, and she moves her lips as if she was speaking—dear me, how odd, she has on a blue dress just like mine!"

"Why, you silly woman, it is your own face that you see!" said the husband, proud of knowing something that his wife didn't know. "That round piece of metal is called a mirror. In the big city everybody has one, although we have not seen them in this country village before."

The wife was charmed with her present and for a few days could not look into the mirror often enough. This was, after all, the first time she had seen a mirror, so, of course, it was the first time she had ever seen the reflection of her own pretty face. But she considered such a wonderful thing far too precious for everyday use, and soon shut it up in its box again and put it away carefully among her most valued treasures.

Years passed, and the husband and wife still lived happily. The joy of their life was their little daughter, who grew up the very image of her mother, and who was so dutiful and affectionate that everybody

90

loved her. Thinking of her own vanity on finding herself so lovely, the mother kept the mirror carefully hidden away, fearing that the use of it might make her little girl conceited.

She never spoke of the mirror, and as for the father he had forgotten all about it. So it happened that the daughter grew up as simple as her mother had been, and knew nothing of her own good looks, or of the mirror which would have reflected them.

But by and by a terrible misfortune befell this happy little family. The good, kind mother fell sick. Although her daughter waited upon her day and night, with loving care, she got worse and worse, until at last there was no doubt that she was dying.

When she found that she must so soon leave her husband and child, the poor woman felt very sorrowful, grieving for those she was going to leave behind, and most of all for her daughter.

She called the girl to her and said, "My darling child, you know that I am very sick. Soon I must die and leave your dear father and you alone. When I am gone, promise me that you will look into this mirror every night and every morning. There you will see me, and know that I am still watching over you." With these words she took the mirror from its hiding place and gave it to her daughter. The girl promised, with many tears, and so the mother, seeming now calm and resigned, died a short time after.

Now this obedient and dutiful daughter never forgot her mother's last request. Each morning and each evening she took the mirror from its hiding place, and looked in it long and earnestly. There she saw the bright and smiling vision of her lost mother. Not pale and sickly as in her last days, but the beautiful young mother of long ago. At night she told her mother the story of the trials and difficulties of the day. In the morning she looked to her mother for sympathy and encouragement in whatever might be in store for her.

So day by day she lived as if she were in her mother's sight, striving still to please her as she had done in her lifetime, and always careful to avoid whatever might pain or upset her.

Her greatest joy was to be able to look in the mirror and say, "Mother, you will be pleased with me today."

Seeing her look into the mirror every night and morning without fail, and seem to converse with it, her father finally asked her the reason for her strange behavior. "Father," she said, "I look in the mirror every day to see my dear mother and to talk with her." Then she told him of her mother's dying wish, and how she had never failed to fulfill it. Touched by so much simplicity, and such faithful, loving obedience, the father shed tears of pity and affection. Nor could he find it in his heart to tell the girl that the image she saw in the mirror was but the reflection of her own sweet face, which was more and more like her dear mother's day by day.

The Fairies' Mallet

THERE were once two farmers who were brothers. Both of them worked hard in planting time and in harvest time. They stood knee-deep in water to plant the young rice, bending their backs a thousand times an hour. They wielded the sickle when the hot sun shone. When the rain poured down in torrents, there they were still at their digging, huddled up in their straw raincoats, for if they did not work, they would have no food to eat.

The elder of the two brothers was named Cho. He worked hard and he was rich. Ever since he was a boy, he had saved his pennies and by now he had a mint of money. He had a big farm, too, and every year he did well, what with his rice, and his silkworms, and his granaries and storehouses. But for all this, he was stingy and miserly, a mean, sour man with not so much as a "good day" and a cup of tea for a wayfarer, or a cake of cold rice for a beggar. His children whimpered when he came near them, and his wife was much to be pitied.

The younger of the two brothers was named Kanè. Unlike his brother, Kanè was as poor as a church mouse. His luck was bad, his silkworms died, and his rice would not flourish. In spite of this he was a merry fellow, a bachelor who loved a song and a cup of *saké*.

His roof, his pipe, his meager supper, all these he would share, very gladly, with anyone. He had a quick wit and the kindest heart in the world. But it is true, though it is a pity all the same, that a man cannot live on love and laughter, and soon Kanè was in a bad way.

"There's nothing to do," he said, "but to swallow my pride" (for he had some) "and go and see if my brother Cho will help me, though I doubt he will do much."

So he borrowed some clothes from a friend for the visit, and set off in a very neat outfit, looking quite the gentleman, and singing a song to keep his courage up.

He saw his brother standing outside his house, and the first minute he thought he was seeing a beggar, for Cho was in such ragged clothes. But soon he called out, "You're early, Cho."

"You're early, Kanè," said Cho.

"May I come in and talk a bit?" asked Kanè.

"Yes," said Cho, "you can, but don't expect me to give you anything to eat, nor to drink at this time of day."

"Very well," said Kanè. "As it happens, it's not food I've come for."

When they were inside the house and sitting down, Cho said, "That's a fine suit of clothes you're wearing, Kanè. You must be doing well. Surely I cannot afford to go about the muddy roads dressed up like a prince. Times are bad, very bad."

In spite of this poor beginning, Kanè plucked up his courage and laughed. And then he said, "Look here, brother. These are borrowed clothes; my own will hardly hold together. My rice crop was ruined, and my silkworms are dead. I have not a *rin* to buy rice seed or new worms. I am at my wits' end, and I have come to you begging. So now you have it. For the sake of our dear mother, give me a handful of seed and a few silkworms' eggs."

At this Cho acted as if he would faint with astonishment and dismay.

"Alack! Alack!" he said. "I am a poor man, a very poor man. Must

94

I rob my wife and my miserable children?" And he moaned and complained like this for half an hour.

But to make a long story short, Cho said that out of brotherly duty, and in honor of their blessed mother, he would sacrifice and give Kanè the silkworms' eggs and the rice. So he got a handful of dead eggs and a handful of musty and moldy rice. "These are no good to man or beast," said the old fox to himself, and he laughed. But to his own brother he said, "Here, Kanè. I'm giving you the best silkworms' eggs and the best rice of all my poor store, and I cannot afford it at all. May the gods forgive me for robbing my poor wife and my children."

Kanè thanked his brother with all his heart for his great generosity, and bowed his head three times. Then off he went, with the silkworms' eggs and rice, skipping and jumping with joy, for he thought that his luck had changed at last. But in the muddy parts of the road he was careful to hold up his pants, for they were borrowed.

When he reached home he gathered some green mulberry leaves. This was to feed the silkworms that he expected to hatch from the dead eggs. And he sat down and waited for the silkworms to come. And come they did, too, and that was very strange, because the eggs were dead eggs for sure. The silkworms were a lively lot. They ate the mulberry leaves in a twinkling, and in no time at all began to wind themselves into cocoons. Kanè was a happy man, and he went out and told his good fortune to all the neighbors. This was where he made his mistake. Then he found a peddler who did his rounds in those parts, and gave him a message to take to his brother Cho, with his compliments and respectful thanks, that the silkworms were doing uncommonly well. This was where he made a bigger mistake. It was a pity he could not let well enough alone.

When Cho heard of his brother's luck he was not pleased. Pretty soon he put on his straw sandals and was off to Kanè's farm. Kanè was out when he got there, but Cho did not care. He went to look at the silkworms. And when he saw how they were beginning to

spin themselves into cocoons, as neat as you please, he took a sharp knife and cut every one of them in two. Then he went home, the bad man!

When Kanè came to look after his silkworms he could not help thinking they looked a bit queer. He scratched his head and said, "It almost appears as though each of them has been cut in half. They seem dead." Then out he went and gathered mulberry leaves. And all those half silkworms began to eat the mulberry leaves, and after that there were twice as many silkworms spinning away as before. And that was very strange, because the silkworms had been dead for sure.

When Cho heard this he went and chopped his own silkworms in two with a sharp knife. But he gained nothing by that, for the silkworms never moved again, but stayed as dead as dead, and his wife had to throw them away the next morning.

After this Kanè planted the rice seed that he had from his brother, and the young rice came up as green as you please and flourished wonderfully.

One day an immense flight of swallows came and settled on Kanè's rice field.

"Arah! Arah!" Kanè shouted. He clapped his hands and beat about with a bamboo stick. So the swallows flew away. In two minutes back they came.

"Arah! Arah!" Kanè shouted, and he clapped his hands and beat about with his bamboo stick. So the swallows flew away. In two minutes back they came.

"Arah! Arah!" Kanè shouted. He clapped his hands and beat about with his bamboo stick. So the swallows flew away. In two minutes back they came.

When he had scared them away for the ninth time, Kanè took his handkerchief and wiped his face. "This is getting to be a habit," he said. But in two minutes back came the swallows for the tenth time. "Arah! Arah!" Kanè shouted, and he chased them over hill and dale, hedge and ditch, rice field and mulberry field, until at last they flew

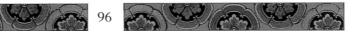

out of sight, and he found himself in a mossy dell shaded by spreading pine trees. He was very tired from running so he lay down upon the moss, and soon fell fast asleep and began snoring.

Then he had a dream. He thought he saw a troop of children come to the mossy glade. The children fluttered here and there among the pine tree trunks. They were as pretty as flowers or butterflies. All of them had dancing bare feet; their hair hung down, long, loose and black; their skin was white like the plum blossom.

For good or for evil, said Kanè to himself, I have seen the fairies' children.

The children finished their dancing and sat down on the ground in a ring. "Leader! Leader!" they cried. "Fetch us the mallet." Then there rose up a handsome boy, about fourteen or fifteen years old, the eldest and the tallest there. He lifted a mossy stone quite close to

Kanè's head. Underneath was a plain little mallet of white wood. The boy took it up and went and stood within the circle of children. He laughed and said, "Now what will you have?"

"A kite, a kite," called out one of the children.

The boy shook the mallet, and lo and behold he shook a kite out of it!—a great kite with a tail on it, and a good ball of twine as well.

"Now what else?" asked the boy.

"A racquet and shuttlecock for me," said a little girl.

And sure enough there they were, a racquet of the best wood, and twenty shuttlecocks, beautifully feathered and gilded.

"Now what else?" said the boy.

"A lot of sweets."

"Greedy!" said the boy, but he shook the mallet, and the sweets appeared.

"A red crêpe frock and a brocade *obi*."

"Miss Vanity!" said the boy, but he shook all this gravely out of the mallet.

"Books, storybooks."

"That's better," said the boy, and out came the books by the dozen, all open to show the lovely pictures.

Now, when the children had their hearts' desires, the leader put the mallet away beneath its mossy stone, and after they had played for some time they became tired and left the mossy dell. Their bright clothes melted away into the gloom of the wood, and their pretty voices grew distant and then were heard no more. It was very still.

Kanè awoke and found the sun setting and darkness beginning to fall. There was the mossy stone right under his hand. He lifted it, and there was the mallet.

"Now," said Kanè, taking it up, "begging the pardon of the fairies' children, I'll be bold and borrow that mallet." So he took it home and spent a pleasant evening shaking gold pieces out of it, and *saké,* and new clothes, and farmers' tools, and musical instruments, and who knows what else!

 98

As you can imagine, pretty soon he became the richest and jolliest farmer in all the countryside. Sleek and fat he grew, and his heart was bigger and kinder than ever.

But what was in Cho's heart when he got wind of all this? Cho turned green with envy, as green as grass. "I'll have a fairy mallet, too," he said, "and be rich for nothing. Why should that idiot spendthrift Kanè have all the good fortune?" So he went and begged rice from his brother, which his brother gave him very willingly, a good sackful. And he waited for it to ripen, quite wild with impatience. It ripened sure enough, and a flight of swallows came and settled upon the good grain.

"Arah! Arah!" shouted Cho, clapping his hands and laughing aloud for joy. The swallows flew away, and Cho was after them. He chased them over hill and dale, hedge and ditch, rice field and mulberry field, until at last they flew out of his sight, and he found himself in a mossy dell shaded by spreading pine trees. Cho looked about him.

"This should be the place," said he. So he lay down and waited with one wily eye shut and one wily eye open.

Soon who should trip into the dell but the fairies' children!

"Leader! Leader! Fetch us the mallet," they cried. Up stepped the leader and lifted away the mossy stone. And behold there was no mallet there!

Now the fairies' children became very angry. They stamped their little feet, and cried and rushed wildly to and fro, and were beside themselves altogether because the mallet was gone.

"See," cried the leader at last, "see this ugly old farmer. He must have taken our mallet. Let us pull his nose for him."

With a shrill scream the fairies' children set upon Cho. They pinched him, and pulled him, and hit him, and set their sharp teeth in his flesh until he yelled in agony. Worst of all, they grabbed his nose and pulled it. It grew long, and longer. It reached his waist. It reached his feet.

 99

Goodness, how the fairies' children laughed! Then they scampered away like fallen leaves before the wind.

Cho cried, and he groaned, and he cursed, and he swore, but his nose did not grow an inch shorter. So, sad and sorry, he gathered it up in his two hands and went to Kanè's house.

"Kanè, I am very sick," said he.

"Indeed, so I see," said Kanè, "a terrible sickness. And how did you catch it?" he asked. And so kind was he that he never laughed at Cho's nose, and there were tears in his eyes at his brother's misfortune. Then Cho's heart melted and he told his brother the whole story, how mean he had been about the dead silkworms' eggs, and everything else. And he asked Kanè to forgive him and to help him out of his misery.

"Wait a minute," said Kanè.

He went to his chest, and brought out the mallet. And he rubbed it very gently up and down Cho's long nose, and sure enough it shortened up very quickly. In two minutes it was back to normal. Cho danced for joy.

Kanè looked at him and said, "If I were you, I'd just go home and try to be different."

When Cho had gone, Kanè sat still and thought for a long time. When the moon rose that night he went out and took the mallet with him. He came to the mossy dell that was shaded with spreading pine trees, and he laid the mallet in its old place under the stone.

"I did not intend," he said, "to steal from the fairies' children."

The Fire Quest

ONE summer night the wise poet sat reading by the light of his candle. The cicada sang in the flower of the pomegranate; the frog sang by the pond. The moon was out and all the stars. The air was heavy and sweet-scented. But the poet was not happy, for moths came by the dozens to the light of his candle; and not just moths, but beetles and dragonflies with their wings rainbow tinted. One and all they came upon the Fire Quest. One and all they burned their bright wings in the flame and so died. And the poet was distressed.

"Little harmless children of the night," he said to them, "why do you still fly upon the Fire Quest? Never, never can you succeed, yet you strive and die. Foolish ones, have you never heard the story of the Firefly Queen?"

The moths and the beetles and the dragonflies fluttered about the candle and ignored him.

"They have never heard the story," said the poet. "Listen:

"The Firefly Queen was the brightest and most beautiful of small things that fly. She lived in the heart of a rosy lotus blossom. The lotus grew on a still lake, and it swayed to and fro while the Firefly Queen slept within. It was like the reflection of a star in the water.

"You must know, oh, little children of the night, that everyone

wished to marry the Firefly Queen. Moths and beetles and dragonflies innumerable flew to the lotus on the lake. And their hearts were filled with passionate love. 'Have pity, have pity,' they cried, 'Queen of the Fireflies, Bright Light of the Lake.' But the Firefly Queen sat and smiled and shone.

"At last she said, 'Oh, you lovers, one and all, why do you gather here idly, cluttering my lotus house? Prove your love, if you love me indeed. Go, and bring me fire, and then I will answer.'

"Then, oh, little children of the night, there was a swift whirr of wings, for the moths and the beetles and the dragonflies innumerable swiftly set out upon the Fire Quest. But the Firefly Queen laughed. Afterward I will tell you the reason for her laughter.

"So the lovers flew here and there in the still night, looking for fire to bring to the Firefly Queen. They found lighted windows and entered. In one room there was a girl who took a love letter from her pillow and read it in tears, by the light of a candle. In another a woman sat holding the light close to a mirror, while she put on her makeup. A great

white moth put out the trembling candle flame with his wings.

" 'Alack! I am afraid,' shrieked the woman; 'the horrible dark!'

"Those that flew on the Fire Quest burned their frail wings in the fire. In the morning they lay dead by the hundreds and were swept away and forgotten.

"The Firefly Queen was safe in her lotus bower with her beloved, who was as bright as she, for he was a great lord of the Fireflies. No need had he to go upon the Fire Quest, for he carried a light beneath his wings.

"And that is how the Firefly Queen tricked her lovers, and why she laughed when she sent them from her on a futile adventure."

"Don't let yourselves be tricked!" cried the wise poet. "Oh, little children of the night, the Firefly Queen is always the same. Give up the Fire Quest and live."

But the moths and the beetles and the dragonflies paid no attention to the words of the wise poet. Still they fluttered about his candle, and they burned their bright wings in the flame and so they died.

Soon, the poet blew out the light. "I will sit in the dark," he said. "It is the only way."